T0194943

THE BOOK LADY

DORIS M. DORWART, ED.D.

authorHOUSE®

AuthorHouse™
1663 Liberty Drive
Bloomington, IN 47403
www.authorhouse.com
Phone: 1 (800) 839-8640

Published by AuthorHouse 06/24/2019

ISBN: 978-1-7283-1689-5 (sc)
ISBN: 978-1-7283-1688-8 (hc)
ISBN: 978-1-7283-1687-1 (e)

Library of Congress Control Number: 2019908446

Print information available on the last page.

ACKNOWLEDGMENTS

While it is almost impossible to identify all the people who have inspired me to write this book, there are bits and pieces of all of you from cover to cover. I have become aware that there are so many true love stories here at Long Community. While the time periods may differ from one romance to another, and the situations range from serious to funny, the one abiding element is love. When I was searching for a name for the perfect lover in my book, Lewis Sabtine recommended his name. Thank you, Lewie.

Since my vision is getting worse with each passing day, this will be my last effort to tell a story. Of course, I know that the world will reel with this news. Thanks to my readers—you made my adventure into writing both fun and amazing.

Do any of you remember your high school English teacher? Well, my editor, Jane Lloyd, is like three English teachers rolled into one. She sometimes sets me crazy with issues like past perfect tense. She has the eyes of an eagle, the patience of Job, and the tenacity of a tiger, when dealing with someone who just wants to tell a story. Jane, I thank you from the bottom of my heart.

CHAPTER 1

Sunday, December 5, 1971

M ARTHA WAS STARTLED when her phone rang. She seldom received calls, unless one of the staff members from the four libraries that she supervised was having a problem, but this was Sunday and the libraries were closed. As she peered out the window, she became aware that it had started to snow. Perhaps Winnie was calling to cancel their usual Sunday church and luncheon routine.

"Hello," Martha said as she sat down on a wing-back chair that was by the front window.

"Miss Harrison, this is Dave Nickles. I hate to bother you, but I have some news that you might like to hear. Remember about three months ago, when you and I were discussing the case of the woman who was murdered and stuffed in a suitcase?"

"Yes," Martha said as she wrinkled her forehead. Dave Nickles was the owner of Nickles Vintage Treasures, her favorite shop.

"Well, anyway, the murdered woman was Dorothy Evans. Even though she was killed years ago, the case is still open. But her family recently made arrangements with me last week to come and pick up some of her belongings. When I got there, they had some furniture, household items, and a large, very old trunk. And I thought you might be interested in what I found," he said excitedly.

"I really don't need a trunk. It would take up too much room in my small duplex."

"Oh, no, not the trunk. It's what I found inside the trunk."

"If you're going to say you found another body, I'll faint," Martha quipped.

Nickles laughed. "My goodness, no. I discovered a drawer at the very bottom of the trunk. That's where I found a photograph album, and right away I thought about you."

Martha was quiet for a moment. "You know what? I think I should at least take a look at it. I'll come right over. Thank you, Mr. Nickles."

She no sooner hung up, than her phone rang again.

"Martha, I'm canceling. I don't like to drive in the snow. If the weather clears up, maybe we could do dinner tonight," Winnie said apologetically.

"I'm taking a quick run to Nickles. He called about finding a photograph album that belonged to Dorothy Evans, you know, that woman they found in a suitcase."

"That gives me the creeps—I wouldn't touch that with a ten-foot pole."

"I'm going to look at it. I may not buy it, but, if it speaks to me, I will," Martha said lightheartedly.

After parking in Nickles' lot, she purposefully ignored the handicap spaces. Treading carefully as she made her way across the macadam, she was pleased to sense that she had handled the slippery surface quite well even with her disability. She hated that term and was surprised that it had even entered her mind. However, when one had one leg shorter than the other, what else could it be labeled? A few days ago, when she had been sitting in the waiting room at the dentist's office, perusing magazines, she had read an article regarding putting mind over body. According to the author, one could overcome physical problems by retraining the mind not to accept the problem.

Martha shook the snow off her cape and entered the shop. Mr. Nickles was on a ladder shelving books. "Good morning, Miss Harrison," he said as he worked his way down. "I put the album on the table by your favorite chair. There are also some new things in the *This and That* room you might fancy." He was always delighted when Martha came in to look over his treasures. Starting his day off by helping such a pretty woman shop was like the icing on a cake.

"Mr. Nickles. you should let Kevin shelve those books. It can be dangerous for you to go up and down on those steps," Martha said as she hurried past the china and bric-a-brac sections to the far end of the shop. She could spend hours in this area. While some might think that many of the items should be tossed out, she could see beauty in every piece. It was here, while she rummaged through all kinds of vintage treasures, that she felt close to her great-aunt Elizabeth. Martha's dad used to tell her stories about his favorite aunt—a beautiful, elegant woman, who loved having her initials prominently displayed on all her possessions. Elizabeth had owned a German silver vanity set that included a hairbrush, a mirror, a fingernail buffer with an ivory handle, and several glass jars to hold lotions and creams. On each of these pieces, a scripted "E" glistened brightly among the engravings. Upon Elizabeth's death, Martha's dad had saved the set and gave it to Martha on her fifth birthday. While her dad had told Martha that the family referred to her as "Betty" sometimes, she always made it known that her name was Elizabeth and would often not reply to any questions until they corrected themselves. Elizabeth had married well, but she was also quite an independent woman with her own views and beliefs. Before Elizabeth had died, she had rewritten her will and had made Martha's dad her only heir. He had used the money to establish a trust fund for his daughter because he wanted her to get an education. This turned out to be a prescient plan because both Martha's parents died when she was only nine years old.

Martha chuckled when she spotted an apron with only one sash attached. A little cast iron turtle, peeking out from between two vases, had been crudely painted but could be turned into a whimsical doorstop. Then, she spotted a badly abused end table with a marble top that was just the right size for her living room. She knew she could make this piece come alive again.

When she saw the album, her heart began to beat just a bit faster. She picked the album up, sat down on the chair, and placed it in her lap. She ran her hands over the cover and wondered how often Dorothy might have done that, too. The album was almost nondescript. There were no embellishments—in fact, it looked quite worn. She felt a warmth—almost like meeting an old friend. It was filled with photographs that had obviously been taken by professionals. As she flipped through the pages, she saw that many of the photos had been signed, *To Dorothy.* On the title page, in elegant calligraphy, were the words *My Friends.* How could one person have so many friends? Martha could count the number of friends she had on one hand. Suddenly, she knew that she had to purchase it. It deserved a home; someone who would take care of it like Dorothy probably had at one time.

A strange feeling came over her. Somehow, she knew that Dorothy wanted her to have this wonderful book.

"By the way," Mr. Nickles said, as he stuck his head around the corner, "congratulations on your promotion. Now that you're Director of Public Libraries for Logan County, I bet your calendar will always be filled with all kinds of activities. That was a nice picture of you in yesterday's paper."

"Thank you. I'm looking forward to organizing our library system. It's a great time to take over the reins, since there are some new and exciting technologies on the horizon that will impact the services our libraries will be able to provide."

"Do you need assistance with anything? I see you found the album."

"I certainly did. I'm fascinated with it and I intend to give it a new home. Oh, I'll also take that unique bronze picture frame," Martha said as she checked her watch. "I want that end table, too, but I won't be able to carry everything. Is Kevin here?"

"Yes, I'll buzz for him. He's in the back getting some items ready to be shipped. Would you like me to put the album and the frame in a shopping bag since it's still snowing?" Mr. Nickles suggested.

"You're always so thoughtful," Martha said as she rummaged through her purse for her wallet.

"Miss Harrison, ever since you bought that lace glove that was torn, I have been wondering what you did with it. If you think I'm nosey, you're right," Mr. Nickle said as he handed her the shopping bag. As Martha was adjusting her cape over her shoulder length, chestnut-colored hair, Nickles was amazed at how beautiful she appeared. But, she didn't seem to realize that she was a beauty; something that set her apart from other pretty women.

Martha smiled. "My neighbor, who does all kinds of needlework, applied her talent closing the hole so perfectly that you can't tell where it had been. Well, anyway, I simply draped it over a slightly-opened drawer on my vanity. I think it looks as if a lady was getting ready to dash to an elegant party. Sounds a bit daffy, doesn't it?"

"Sounds great to me. You have such a wonderful, gentle attitude. No wonder you always appear to be happy."

"Good morning, Miss Harrison," Kevin said as he came around the corner. "I'll be happy to carry your purchases to your car."

After Kevin placed Martha's items in her car, he suddenly asked, "Miss Harrison, do you know the Rod Stewart song, *Maggie May*?"

"I know of it, but I don't know any of the lyrics."

"You really need to listen to them the next time you hear that song," the young man advised. Suddenly, his face turned red and he hurried back into the shop.

As she drove away, she thought about what Mr. Nickles had said about her always being happy. She couldn't remember when she truly had felt happy. But then again, she had been living in a make-believe world for so long, she wasn't certain that she could ever actually function in a real one.

As soon as she got home, she called Winnie. "Well, I have to confess; I went to Nickles and bought a few things. And, before you ask, yes, I bought the album."

"I wouldn't want a dead woman's album in my house. There may be blood on it. And, worse yet, there could be a spell on the damned thing," Winnie said hesitantly.

"Now, Winnie, there won't be any blood on it. As far as having a spell, there's no such thing. The items I got will fit into my place just fine."

"Honey, where are you going to put more stuff?"

"I'll find space. Kevin helped me load my trunk. I got an end table that has a marble top. It was a buy," Martha said excitedly.

"Oh, the table was probably just an excuse for you to get that good-looking Kevin alone on the parking lot," Winnie teased.

"Talking about Kevin—he asked me what I thought about Rod Stewart's song, *Maggie May.*"

"What was your reply?" Winnie prodded.

"I said something like, 'I heard the song, but I didn't know the lyrics.'"

"Woman, you were being hit on. That song is about a young man who falls in love with an older woman. He was testing you," Winnie explained.

"What! You've got to be kidding," Martha said. "Kevin is probably seventeen. My God, he's in high school."

"You may know a lot about books and libraries, but, when it comes to the dating game, you need lessons," Winnie said with a laugh.

"I may not have been on a date for a while, but, believe me, Kevin will not be on my dance card."

"Talking about dancing—do you plan on going to the Holiday Hop? If you are, why not wear the sash that belonged to your Aunt Elizabeth—you know—the one that has a precious dance card attached?"

"Yes, I do, but I'll be going alone. County employees are expected to attend. Our latest newsletter just about spelled that out. So, I'll be going. I'm not sure about wearing the sash. I'm not certain yet what I'll be wearing."

"Don't forget to wear the lifts in your shoes. Better yet, wear those wedges you had made because you'll certainly have offers to dance. Why didn't you invite someone to go along? What about that guy who just opened the new coffee shop? I hear he's single and handsome," Winnie offered. "Oh, you also have someone right under your nose and I hear he's—"

"No more talk about dating—or those ugly shoes. Okay?"

One way or the other, Winnie would get a date for Martha. She knew how to bring people together. Martha wouldn't know what hit her. She shuddered when she shifted her thoughts to the album again. Martha was her friend and she didn't want anything bad to happen to her. But buying that album was wrong. If Winnie ever got the opportunity, she would destroy the album. One woman, brutally murdered, and stuffed into a suitcase was one too many. We don't need another one.

CHAPTER 2

Sunday, December 7, 1941

30 years before...

FERN HAD MANAGED to change her nightgown and climb back into bed before another contraction hit. Her sister, Ivy, had called Eunice, the midwife; and Fern's husband, Charlie, who had volunteered to help a neighbor build a garage, was on his way home. Doctor Johnson was out of town so he wouldn't be available for the delivery. Fern would have to count on Eunice to bring her baby into the world.

"You should have gone to Weaverville last month. I wanted you out of these godforsaken hills before the baby arrived. This is like living in the middle of nowhere. There's nothing but trees and more trees. Next thing you'll be planting flowers and stuff. You just won't listen to anyone who gives you advice, will you?" Ivy's sharp tongue seemed to bounce all around the pretty bedroom.

"The doctor had planned on being here. But my baby decided it was time to come out and meet her mom," Fern said sweetly, ignoring Ivy's whining voice.

"There were lots of other places you could have found a

9

house. Logan County has a great low-rent building right down town," Ivy argued.

"My Charlie loves it here. He can go fishing, or hunting, or even skiing. This area has lots of streams and lakes and is ideal for people who want a quiet life. We don't want to live in the noisy city," Fern explained.

"You never should have gotten pregnant in the first place, Fern. You knew the risks involved in having a child so late in life," Ivy scolded as she took a seat on the old rocking chair alongside Fern's bed. "Of course, you didn't listen to me as usual," Ivy sighed as she saw Fern grip the bedcovers. "I've heard some terrible things about babies born to older women—just terrible."

"Ivy, please. Everything's going to be alright. Eunice has delivered lots of babies. And, my little one will be just fine. Wait and see," Fern said. She glanced at her older sister and saw that her arms were crossed over her stomach and a deep frown dominated her face.

"Don't use that tone of voice with me. You know better than that. I don't know what's become of this world. No one has respect any more. With all the talk of war, they are just trying to scare people. Even the President, when he addressed the nation the other week, made it sound as if we'll be in the center of things before you know it. My Harry's been talking about enlisting, but I have forbidden him to do such a silly thing," Ivy said.

"Harry's old enough to do that. He doesn't need your permission," Fern reminded her sister as she began breathing harder.

"In my house he does. I said **no** and I meant it," Ivy said sharply.

Suddenly, Eunice came bounding up the stairs. "We're

at war, ladies. They just announced that the Japanese have bombed Pearl Harbor."

"Where the hell's Pearl Harbor?" Ivy asked angrily.

"Hawaii," Eunice said.

"I don't understand any of this. Why did they do that?" Ivy challenged.

"Oh, the baby...the baby's coming," Fern said as she gritted her teeth.

Eunice flew into action. She hurriedly gave directions to Fern.

Less than twenty minutes later, Fern took a deep breath and the baby slid into Eunice's hands. "You have a little girl," Eunice announced happily as she carefully cleaned the baby and laid her in Fern's arms.

Fern pulled back the blanket and slowly counted the baby's fingers and toes. "See, Ivy, my precious little baby is fine." Fern tucked the blanket around the infant just as a little tear rolled down her face. She laughed as the baby opened and closed her little fist.

"Have you made up your mind what the baby's name will be? You know our grandmother wants you to call her Dandelion," Ivy reminded her sister.

"I know she wanted all her grandchildren to have names of growing things, but I am not going to do that. Her name will be Martha, and that's that."

Ivy's retort was interrupted by the slamming of the front door. Charlie Harrison came hurrying up the stairs—making a raucous noise as his heavy steel-tipped work boots hit each uncarpeted step. "Fern, my precious Fern, are you okay? And who's that lying in your arms," Charlie said as he grinned from ear to ear.

"Meet your daughter, Martha."

DORIS M. DORWART, Ed.D.

Charlie leaned down and kissed his wife on her forehead.

"God, she's beautiful—just like her mom," Charlie said. "See, Ivy, you were sure that there would be something wrong with her. Why, she's a beautiful child. Thank goodness she takes after her mother and not me," Charlie said as he chuckled. "She's absolutely perfect!"

"Wait and see. Wait and see. We can't see inside her head," Ivy said ominously.

"Ivy, I think you need to leave. You're not happy because our baby is fine. What a piece of work you are," Charlie said as he turned his back on his sister-in-law.

As Ivy went down the stairs, she murmured, "The war is a sign. The baby was born and bombs fell."

"Charlie, I'll stay here to help with Fern and Martha until morning. Then I think we can get one of the nurses from town to come during the day." As Eunice stripped the bed and took blankets from the cedar chest to cover Fern, she asked, "Why did Japan bomb Pearl Harbor? What did we do?"

"The announcer on the radio explained that Pearl Harbor is an extremely large US naval base with lots of vessels. Japan wanted to seize the Dutch East Indies and Malaya, but, with such a major naval presence in the Pacific, they needed to clear the way. In order to capture Southeast Asia, the Japanese needed to get rid of our force in Hawaii. I didn't hear everything he said, but I'm certain we'll hear much more. Oh, one thing the newscaster said was that he thought that the war would be over in a few weeks." Charlie paused, pulled his eyebrows together and said, "I'd like to believe he's right. I'd hate to think I brought a child into a world of war. Only time will tell."

After his wife had fallen asleep, Charlie, in his stocking feet, hurried down the stairs to the living room. He put his chair in front of the radio and turned the volume down. President Roosevelt was speaking:

"Our enemies have performed a brilliant feat of deception, perfectly timed and executed with great skill."

Charlie pulled out a big red handkerchief from his overalls and covered his face. He allowed himself to weep. On what should have been a joyous day, a nation, far across the sea, didn't care that Charlie had just been given a child.

CHAPTER 3

Tuesday, December 7, 1971

M ARTHA ARRIVED AT the Logan East Branch Public Library just as the large clock that had stood on the lawn for many years was striking seven. Since she had invited a guest speaker today, she wanted to make certain that everything was organized properly. Before Martha was promoted, she had been the director of this branch. She took a moment to remind herself that now Molly Miller was in charge of this facility. Two students from the library club at the local high school had been working on a display about Pearl Harbor for more than three weeks—Martha was a stickler for perfection. After she hung up her cape, she turned her attention to the display and was pleased to see that an enlarged photograph of two nurses, running towards a navy vessel, would be bound to catch the attention of guests. The display included books, articles, photos and even a model of the *USS Arizona*, a fully staffed battleship that was heavily damaged by the Japanese.

In June, when Martha had attended the American Library Association's Conference in Dallas, she had met Kate Hendricks, the speaker for today's event. When she had asked her if she would consider coming to Logan County to make a presentation, she had readily agreed. As an army nurse,

Kate had lived through that cowardly attack and Martha was looking forward to hearing her presentation. She hoped that she would be able to handle what she was about to hear since she normally avoided anything that dealt with Pearl Harbor. It was time that she stop giving power to her deceased Aunt Ivy, a harbinger of doom and gloom, and join the grown-up world.

It suddenly crossed Martha's mind that today she would turn thirty. She hoped that none of her staff would remember it since she had long ago given up celebrating on this day. Like her mother, Martha had been willing to accept December 8th as her birthday; somehow it just made things easier.

Whenever she was alone, which was most of the time, she felt that the whole Pearl Harbor tragedy was her fault. She could only remember snippets of her life before she had had to live with Aunt Ivy, but those little memories always gave her hope that her world would become happier. However, she was more certain than ever that her limp was some type of punishment. Once again, her thoughts shifted to her Aunt Ivy. Martha thought of her aunt as poison ivy since there was little in life that Ivy liked. Her aunt's thick, unruly eyebrows reminded her of the gardener's rhyme, *"Hairy vine, and no friend of mine."* Her aunt's constant unkind comments to a young Martha had spread like a rash—normal for poison ivy. Martha always wanted her aunt to be like Ivy Lillian Wallace, her favorite childhood author, who wrote stories about Pookie, a little white furry rabbit. Her only comfort came when she made herself a promise that someday she would escape her aunt.

Martha had lost both her parents when she was only nine. She was immediately moved to Aunt Ivy's house, where she remained until she graduated from college, thanks to the trust fund that her parents had arranged for her. She hated her aunt's house. It was devoid of anything bright and cheerful. The house looked neglected, and it cried out for some fresh paint. The yard was ignored and untended and only the hardiest—or the most obdurate—of plants managed to survive the lack of care. Those that did endure were straggly, scrawny and anemic. So, when she was in the market for a place to call her own, Martha kept looking until she found one that had room for plants and flowers in the yard.

The sound of voices brought her back to the present. As the staff began to arrive at the library, she steadied herself, and realized that she must get through this day; after all, she was the director of the four county public libraries. Molly Miller hurried through the doorway as she clutched a large bouquet of roses in her arms.

"Good morning, Martha. I got these roses for you to present to our speaker. I'll put them in a vase in my office," she said as she scurried away.

By the time Kate arrived at noon, Martha felt that the jitters were gone and the competent *manager persona* was ready. As Kate walked in, she noticed Martha and immediately greeted her warmly. While Kate was no longer in the service, she looked smart in her stylish navy blue suit and white silk blouse. Martha introduced Molly to Kate and allowed Molly to take over.

Soon after, Molly took the mic in hand and turned to the audience. "Ladies and gentlemen, welcome to our commemorative program about Pearl Harbor. While we often hear about the attack on December 7, 1941, we don't often have the privilege of learning about it from someone who was stationed at Pearl Harbor as a nurse. Kate Hendricks was there on that tragic day. Kate, we're grateful that you survived and honored to have you as our speaker."

As the audience welcomed Kate, Martha took a seat in the back of the room. She was not feeling well. She motioned for Molly to come to her side and whispered, "Molly, I may have to leave. If that happens, please take charge of ending our activity by inviting everyone to tour your library."

"Thank you for inviting me to be with you today. I plan on giving you a quick summary of the attack to set the scene, and then I'll take questions regarding the role that the nurses played in assisting the wounded and the impact it had on us. It was Sunday, December 7, 1941. Sundays were always laid-back and quiet times for all of us. My friend Lois and I got on our bikes and decided to visit the Botanical Gardens. We both had our cameras slung over our shoulders and took little notice of the noise coming from the skies. When we heard the roar of planes, we thought our boys were conducting training maneuvers." Kate paused, took a deep breath, and then said, "As we were about to enter the gardens, a military policeman riding a horse, approached and ordered us to return to our stations immediately since we were under attack by the Japanese."

Kate leaned against the edge of a desk and said quietly, "Suddenly, there was a tremendous explosion and black smoke was shooting high into the sky. It was obvious that it was coming from Battleship Row. I grabbed Lois just as a second explosion came. Peddling as fast as we could, we hurried back to our stations. We didn't know it at the time, but the first bomb had breached the *Arizona's* forward magazine, the ammunition room, and the crew of over 1,000 never had a chance. We knew from the mayhem and the black, black smoke that there were going to be hundreds of casualties."

The audience members were spellbound—silence reigned. Kate looked upwards, sighed and said, "The bombs and strafing didn't stop. The three hundred nurses that were stationed at Pearl flew into action to care for the injured. The Japanese planes came in waves. We learned much later that the Japanese had managed to maneuver their vessels and planes across the Pacific by zigzagging through the shipping lanes. The attack was, indeed, not expected. I can still see the red circles displayed on the wings of the Japanese planes. Even though the *Arizona* had listed into the ocean, and she knew that her boyfriend Carl was aboard, Lois was able to maintain her sanity and fulfilled her duties as a nurse."

Martha shifted in her seat. Her stomach began to rumble even louder.

"The attack," Kate said, "began a little after seven and lasted for about two hours. The first group of 183 planes was merciless. Then another 167 planes joined the incredible assault. In spite of being under a surprise attack, our military was able to begin their defense in less than fifteen minutes, and they were able to take down some of the planes. While the Japanese also had planned to destroy our aircraft carriers, fortunately, they had been moved out to sea for training. However, they were able to discover many of our planes parked wingtip to wingtip, at various airfields."

Kate paused for a few moments. She folded her hands and quietly said, "More than 2,500 people, including civilians, were killed and many, many more were wounded. One memory that I simply cannot erase from my mind is when Lois snapped a picture of the *Arizona* and she was screaming at the same time."

Martha began to feel light-headed. She just couldn't listen to any more, so she quietly slid off her chair and hurried to her former office.

For a few moments, Katie was stoic. Out of the corner of

her eye, she saw that Martha had left the room. She took this as a signal that she should wrap-up her talk. Then she said, "Any questions?"

An elderly gentleman, sitting in the last row, raised his hand. "You are to be congratulated, ma'am. Since you were there, and witnessed death around you, do you have any sense that something like that could happen again?"

"That's a great question. I would like to think that the Pearl Harbor attack was a lesson for the world. However, there are still many areas of unrest and political uprisings that should be quelled. At the same time, we have also seen some remarkable things happen this past year. For instance, the first heart and lung transplant was performed. We saw astronauts walk on the moon. Ironically, while we greeted these achievements with joy, thousands of people fled from the war in Pakistan. I would like to assure you that nations will resolve problems without guns and bombs, but I can't do that. What we can do is choose our leaders wisely, act as one nation, and respect and honor even those who do not look like us. I hope you enjoyed the presentation today and I want to thank Miss Harrison for inviting me. I love to visit libraries. Being surrounded by all these books makes me want to read all of them. I wish I had the time but that would be impossible."

"Earlier, I asked Miss Harrison what book was the best seller of all times. Now, if you think you know the answer, please raise your hand and, if you are correct, you'll get a certificate for dinner for two at Bob's Restaurant. By the way, Bob happens to be an old college friend."

The old man in the last row raised his hand again. "I believe the book was the *New English Bible*. I understand that a million copies were sold in just one day. That might give us all some hope for the future. I hesitate to ask, but was Bob a beau?"

"Not exactly. But I can tell you he's married and has five kids. So I guess he's over me," Kate said as she chuckled.

The laughter that filled the room spilled down the hall into the office. Martha heard the laughter coming from the main library room, but, for now, she needed to be alone—alone with her sadness and her feelings of guilt.

❧ CHAPTER 4 ❧

December 11, 1971

M ARTHA ROLLED OVER in bed and pulled the covers up to her neck. She had had a restless night. No matter what she had tried, sleep had alluded her. After a few minutes more, she finally gave up and got out of bed. It was her Saturday off and she had nothing planned to fill her day except for the Holiday Hop that the county commissioners were holding that evening.

After making a pot of coffee, she poured herself a cup. When she glanced at the album that was lying on the kitchen table, she thought about the ornate frame that she also had purchased. Perhaps she could find a photo in the album that would be appropriate. The frame was so different that she wanted to put it on the end table that she purchased; that is, as soon as it was refinished. Pulling the cover of the album back, it automatically opened to a page where there was a sepia photo of a smiling handsome man with beautiful teeth, who looked to be in his late twenties. The photo was signed *To Dorothy with love*. What a lucky girl Dorothy must have been to have had such a gorgeous man love her. She removed the photo carefully and was pleased to discover that it fit the frame exactly.

While she wished she didn't have to attend the Holiday Hop tonight, she knew that the commissioners expected all their employees to be a part of the festivities. She assumed that most people would arrive in couples. But she also knew that there were other ladies who would probably come alone. And, after all, Martha was used to escorting herself. She planned to bide her time chatting with people and being polite, but, when she was finished with her meal, she would discreetly leave the building.

She chose her outfit very carefully. She wanted to look elegant, but not as if she were out on the prowl. Finally, choosing a long black crepe skirt with a slit that didn't expose too much leg, a white long-sleeved silk blouse, she stood before the full-length mirror. She realized that something was missing. A belt—it was then that she remembered the cloth-covered box of belts and sashes that had belonged to Aunt Elizabeth. After pulling it down from her closet shelf, her eyes caught a glimpse of one of her favorites—a hand-crocheted sash with embedded pearls. This one was dramatic; elegant but simple. Elizabeth must have worn it frequently. Martha tied it around her waist and twisted and turned in front of the mirror again. Finally, she said, "Okay, that's enough."

Then, she thought about her shoes. Winnie had recommended that she wear the wedges that were custom-made for her just a few months ago that took away the limp. She held them up and shook her head. She felt that they were the ugliest shoes she had ever seen. Opening a box that held a pair of shoes that were nothing more than narrow straps of black patent leather, she sighed and immediately wanted to wear them. While the heels were less than one inch high, she knew that, if she wore them tonight, she would have to rely on trying to hold herself upright without limping by standing on her toes.

Later that evening, as she entered the ballroom at the Eden Hotel, she was surprised to see that there was a welcoming committee greeting everyone as they entered. She was grateful that she knew everyone's name and was pleased to see that guests were being ushered to their tables.

"Welcome, I'll be your usher. Please follow me. I love your blouse, Miss Harrison," Hannah, the secretary for the commissioners' office, said. "It looks so elegant."

"Thank you, Hannah." Martha said as she followed her to a table for ten.

"Miss Harrison, Commissioner Lewis Holmes personally requested that you were to be seated at his table. He should be here shortly." Martha instantly thought about Sherlock Holmes, one of her favorite literary sleuths.

Now, Martha thought, now is the time that I need to get nervous. She had met him only one time but had liked him immediately. No one seemed to know much about him except that he was single. He was appointed to fill a ten-month vacancy because one commissioner had moved to Florida. She cautioned herself not to make too much of his asking for her to be seated at his table. Perhaps he wasn't aware of her disability. She had been disappointed too many times when it came to gentlemen whom she might have liked to get to know. She spied him coming to the table with Hannah and she swallowed hard.

"Miss Harrison," Lewis said as he pulled out the chair beside her. "I'm so pleased that you decided to come to our celebration. May I say that you look superb tonight?" Lewis said as he smiled broadly.

"Thank you, Mr. Holmes," Martha said nervously.

"Whoa. Please call me Lewis. I have a few friends who'll be joining us shortly. I'm sure you'll like them. And, if you don't, I'll just chase them away."

"Who will you chase away, Lewis?" said a lady with golden curls piled high on the top of her head.

"Not you, Joyce. Martha, I'd like to introduce you to my sassy cousin Joyce. Martha is head of the public library system of our county and does a fantastic job," Lewis said as he patted Martha's hand.

As his other guests arrived, Lewis introduced Martha to each of them. Martha had never been treated so royally and she was enjoying herself tremendously. Surprisingly, Martha found herself included in many of the conversations. The guests asked lots of questions about books and topics involving the county.

After the meal was over, the emcee announced that the hop would open with the traditional waltz contest. He said, "This contest is limited to one couple per table. The gentleman whose birthday is closest to the date when our office first opened on March 15th, must choose a partner. Also, there is a card on your table with the table number; this must go on the back of the gentleman's jacket so the judges can identify a winner more easily."

Lewis turned to Martha and said, "Martha, may I have the pleasure of dancing with you?" Nervously, Martha stood up and he guided her to the dance floor. "I'm not the best dancer, Martha. I'll try not to embarrass you."

"Are you aware that I—"

"Yes. You have a little leg problem. I'm aware of that, Martha. Now take my hand and let's dance."

Martha could feel his hand on her waist. He was a good head taller than she and his shoulders were broad. His dark hair lay in waves, creating an ideal frame for his rugged face. She was very aware how gently he held her hand. She could smell the aroma of his cologne and it was mesmerizing her. She thought that if she wished hard enough, the orchestra would go on playing forever.

This was a *first* for Martha, and she could hardly believe that she had allowed herself to feel this way. Her wonderful sensations were jolted when she suddenly heard the roar of a gunshot. Almost immediately, Martha found herself flat on the floor with Lewis' body on top of her. "Don't move," he said calmly. "Lie perfectly still. There might be another shot."

People were screaming, and knocking over chairs as they tried to get out of the ballroom. It seemed like forever until it quieted down. Lewis tried to reassure Martha by whispering in her ear, "It'll be alright, Martha."

"There he goes. He's in the balcony," someone yelled. Others were directing people to the doorways while expounding, "Call 911!"

Meanwhile, four men dressed in uniforms with SF logos on their sleeves dashed up the staircase to the balcony. When they got to the top of the stairs, the lead officer turned around and yelled "Force 5!"

Lewis rolled off Martha and scanned the scene. He took Martha's hands and got her to her feet. "Hold on to my arm, Martha, and I'll guide you to the table. The shooter is gone now, I can assure you of that. He's on the run." His words calmed her.

Just then, a man came over to Lewis and whispered into his ear, "We don't know how he got in, boss, but they're chasing him now. The balcony's clear. He might have been here since yesterday."

Lewis nodded his head and then turned immediately to Martha. "I hope I didn't hurt you. I only wanted to protect you."

"You may have saved my life," she responded, almost in a whisper.

"Whoever that shooter was, if he really wanted to kill someone, I don't think he would have missed. It could have been a warning to someone, and we think we might know who it was. There was a case of domestic violence yesterday and the man had threatened to shoot his wife. In all probability, he wanted to warn her," Lewis said, hoping he could convince Martha that all was well.

As the room quieted down a bit, the emcee got back on the mic, "Folks, we got the all clear signal. The building is safe. Please, return to your tables." The orchestra began to play again. When Lewis saw his cousin, he waved to her and she came running over.

"My God, Lewis, what was that?" she said as she tried to put her curls back into place. "Was anyone hurt?"

"No. The police are on it, Joyce. There was a report yesterday that a man threated his wife with a gun. They're on his tail. The building is safe," Lewis said as he tried to calm his sister down.

"Well, we're leaving," she said as she and her husband hurried out.

"Martha, I'll leave it up to you. Would you like to leave or would you prefer to stay awhile and dance?" Lewis asked.

"Let's dance," she said sweetly as Lewis took her hand.

When they finally heard the strains of *Goodnight, Ladies*, Lewis led Martha back to the table. "What do you say we take a run over to Jack's Diner for a cup of coffee?"

"I have my car here," Martha said.

Lewis put his hand up and a man, who had been standing

on the side, came over immediately. "Martha, this is Rocco. He'll drive your car home. Meanwhile, we can get to know one another a bit better."

Martha put the keys in Rocco's hand and said, "Just put them in the letter slot in my front door, please. Thank you very much."

In less than twenty minutes, Martha and Lewis had large mugs of coffee in front of them. They were the only two customers in the diner.

"Martha, you're certainly not what I thought a librarian would look like."

"Oh, no, not you, too," she said. "Everyone thinks we should have a bun on the back of our heads and wire-rimmed glasses perched on the end of our noses," Martha responded as she laughed.

"When I went to school, we had a librarian who could have been a stand-in for Quasimodo! You are too beautiful to hide behind all those books."

"I really don't hide behind them, but I do read lots of them. My dad used to take me to the little local library every Saturday. He would sit at one of the library tables with lots of books in front of him, while I entertained myself in the children's section. It was an unassertive brick building, but for the four, half Ionic columns on its façade that would make me feel as if I were entering a place that was almost sacred. I pretended that I was entering Athena's temple. Everything was neat and tidy. It was a safe place. After getting to know the librarian, I fell in love with the whole library scene and I had a recurring dream of becoming a librarian."

"What's your favorite classic and why?" Lewis asked.

"Oh, that's a difficult question to answer. But, if I have to choose one, it would be *Wuthering Heights*."

"Ah ha, you're a romantic, I see."

"There are those who don't classify that book as a love story. For instance, my friend Winnie is adamant that it's a book about revenge. But I simply cannot accept that. Some see it as a gothic novel. Some serious readers classify it as a novel in the Romantic philosophy that was so popular at the time both here and in England. Of course, the book is filled with raw emotions: the kind that many people experience, but the entire story is supported with passionate, deep-seated love. Why, the love story continues into eternity and you can't beat that for true love."

"You have to admit, though, the lovers in the book did some strange things. Heathcliff is crazy about Catherine, but he comes to understand that she can't marry him because of his low status. And, the guy runs away so she marries someone else. Go figure!"

"Catherine had plans to help Heathcliff raise his status, but he didn't know that," Martha argued. "Catherine and Heathcliff are soul mates. They're only happy and complete when they are together in the natural world—high in the tors or on the wild moors. Wouldn't it be ideal to find your perfect partner...to find the person who completes you?"

"He should have stayed and fought for his lady love," Lewis said as he was leaning on his elbows, staring at Martha. "I heard your every word, believe me, I did. But what amazes me are your gorgeous green eyes." He reached across the table and took both of her hands in his.

"Thank you, Lewis," Martha said as she blushed. "Do you bring all your dates to this diner?"

"No. I only bring good-looking women with green eyes here," Lewis teased. He made a mental note that it was time that he read *Wuthering Heights* again. "Diners have always fascinated me. Look around, Martha. Can't you picture the ghosts that probably haunt this place? Maybe a proposal of marriage. Oh, look. Those men who just came in. They're hunched over in that back booth. Probably plotting a murder or two or three. But I bet they're not discussing *Wuthering Heights.*"

"Lewis, you should be a writer. What an imagination you have!"

"When my mom was feeling fine, she would take me to the library to look at picture books. The lady there was always so kind and loving that I wanted to go there every day. I called her *The Book Lady.* I think she was my first love."

"How precious. As a librarian, I always try to help children develop a love for reading. Thank you for sharing that with me, Lewis."

"I've a question to ask you, my beautiful Martha. Will you be my date for New Year's Eve? I've been invited to a black tie event hosted by Mr. Ronald Worthington—you know, the guy who owns half this town."

Martha looked at Lewis for a moment and then, surprising herself, she quickly replied, "Lewis, I would love to be your New Year's Eve date."

⋘ CHAPTER 5 ⋙

December 12, 1971

EARLY THE NEXT morning, Winnie sat in her car until she thought she saw movement in Martha's house. Then, she hurriedly ran up the front steps and impatiently rang the bell. She had heard about the shooting at the Holiday Hop at Eden Hotel and couldn't wait to be certain that her friend was safe. When the door opened and she saw Martha standing there in her pajamas, she threw her arms around her and started to cry.

"You're okay, you're okay," she sobbed.

Martha stroked Winnie's hair and said, "Come in. Yes, I'm fine. Let's go into the kitchen. I'll make coffee."

Winnie dug into her large handbag and retrieved some tissues. "I want to hear everything—everything. Don't leave anything out."

"Okay, but stop crying. Okay?"

"I was going to call you, but then I wasn't sure that that would be the right thing to do and then I......."

"Winnie, Winnie, drink your coffee. Let me talk," Martha encouraged.

As Winnie calmed down, Martha said, "When I got to the

Eden Hotel, there was a receiving line and I was escorted to Lewis' table."

"Lewis?"

"The newest commissioner, Lewis Holmes. He had requested that I be seated at his table." Winnie tried to interrupt. "Now, be quiet, or this will take all day. After the meal, the entertainment began with a waltz contest and Lewis asked me to be his partner." Winnie's eyes opened wide. "As we were dancing, there was a gunshot."

"Oh, my, God," Winnie said as she grabbed Martha's arm.

"Before I knew anything, I was flat on the floor with Lewis on top of me."

"Say what?" Winnie exclaimed loudly.

"There was a great deal of yelling and screaming, but all turned out very well. No one was hurt. Lewis believes that it was a man, who had been involved in a domestic violence incident the day before, when he had threatened to shoot his wife."

"Did they catch him?"

"I'm not sure of that. Lewis said that it was nothing that I should worry about."

"Am I hearing a different tone in your voice?" Winnie asked.

"What do you mean?"

"When you say 'Lewis', somehow you sound different," Winnie explained.

"I do?"

"Are you going to see him again?"

"Yes. In fact, I'm going to go to a New Year's Eve party with him," Martha said as she felt a smile forming. "Oh, I forgot, we went to Jack's Diner and…"

"I thought you drove your car to the Eden?"

"Well, I did. But one of Lewis' friends drove my car home and even parked it in my garage," Martha said coyly.

"One other question: Did he kiss you?"

"Winnie! My goodness."

"Well, did he?"

When her phone rang, Martha felt relief. "Hello," she said in a relaxed tone.

"Switzerland? My goodness, Lewis—When?—this afternoon—the party will be at Bella Luna? Wow, that scares me a bit—I realize that I'll be with you—Mrs. Worthington wants me to attend a tea on the 27th—But I've never been to the mansion—Oh, you'll be home on the 27th and you'll pick me up—Yes, Lewis—This all sounds so exciting—Me too, Lewis—Merry Christmas."

Winnie was on the edge of her seat. Her eyes were fixated on Martha's face.

For a few moments, Martha was silent. "Oh my, Winnie. I'm going to need help in finding the right clothes. And, oh, Winnie, do you think I'll fit into this kind of society?"

"You'll do fine. A well-educated woman like you—they'll fall in love with you, I guarantee it. It's time to go shopping!"

"Let's put the shopping off until Saturday. I have lots to do here at home to get ready for a staff meeting this week. I must develop goals and benchmarks for each of my directors. Will you be able to do it then?"

"Sure. I'll get out of here so you can finish your work. Martha, you are one lucky, lucky lady."

"Why?"

"Because you have me. Now, answer my question—did he kiss you?"

"Yes."

As Winnie drove away, she suddenly remembered that damned album. She wasn't sure she could actually steal something from her friend. But this situation was different— it could be a life or death situation.

⟡ CHAPTER 6 ⟡

December 13, 1971

M ARTHA WASN'T SURE that she could get herself together in order to conduct her staff meeting today. Attending a New Year's Eve party at the mansion and having tea with Mrs. Worthington might weigh so heavily on her mind that she might forget that she must live in the real world.

This would be the first time that she would be meeting with her staff in her new county office. Pleased that they were all on time, and chatting while they waited for her, Martha pushed her chair away from the desk so she could get closer to her staff. All four branch directors were seated in a small circle, and they moved over to make room for her. She recently had become aware of the awesome responsibilities that she had taken on when she agreed to be the Director of Public Libraries for Logan County. For many years, the county had functioned with four libraries, each with a separate director. Now, however, the commissioners wanted to meld the activities and programs that the four libraries offered the residents of the county.

"The purpose of this meeting today is to introduce you to a new routine, regarding how you manage your library as part of a system and how and when you act as one library.

The packets I prepared for you will give you all the goals that the commissioners have given us. Stanley, Susan, and Gwen: You have all been directors of your libraries for several years and most of your responsibilities will not change. However, when it comes to preparing annual budgets, you'll submit your requests to me and we'll work out any problems that I might find. You'll be expected to gather the same data as before, and I'll use your figures when I prepare the system budget."

"While I've been your assistant at this library for two years, I'm unfamiliar with all the duties that a director must fill," Molly said.

"Don't worry. You and I will spend some quality time going over the new tasks you'll be assuming."

"Martha, does that mean that a particular branch can't offer something that other branches don't?" Stanley Barber, Director of the South Branch asked.

"No. As long as we can verify that that program is needed by those who use your branch. If others need that resource, too, then we must make sure that they are able to participate in one way or another. I'll be meeting with each one of you individually every month. I'll also hold system meetings to give you ample opportunity to learn from one another."

Susan Yost, Director of the West Branch asked, "I've been concerned for quite some time that my branch gets overlooked many times."

"We don't do that, do we?" an annoyed Gwen Preston, Director of the North Branch asked.

"I have the smallest collection and my environment is bland when compared to the other branches," Susan argued.

"Ah, that's something we could focus on when we submit the library grants to the State Library," Martha said. "We'll need to work on collecting the kind of data we need to verify that."

"I'd like that," Susan replied.

"Since I'm the newest director here, and I'll be following in Martha's impressive footsteps, I'll need time to get my feet wet a bit longer before I can establish my goals for the East Branch," Molly said nervously.

"You did an excellent job with our guest speaker. Take your time forming your goals and, if you want to contact the other directors, please feel free to do so," Martha said.

"Before I forget," Stanley said, "something unusual happened in my library a few days ago. A heavy-set man approached me and began asking lots of personal questions about you. He made me feel apprehensive."

"What kind of questions?" Martha asked.

"Oh, like how old you were, if you had a boyfriend, and oh, other personal stuff that I can't remember. He gave me the chills, so I brushed him off. I tried to see what kind of car he left in, but he seemed to disappear. He was just plain creepy," Stanley said as he shivered.

"Keep me posted, Stanley. Let me know if he returns."

"One more thing about him—he was looking through the cabinet, where we keep the old church records, and was taking notes. But, he sure didn't look like a person who belonged in my library," Stanley said, as he wrinkled his nose.

"Be careful, Stanley, you know we can't put any restrictions on who uses our resources. You may want to consider moving that cabinet so it's more in line with your vision," Martha recommended.

The discussion was interrupted by a delivery man, holding a long, narrow flower box. "I'm looking for *The Book Lady*."

Molly jumped up and said, "That has to be you. I'll get

them for you, Martha. I bet someone's congratulating you on your promotion."

"What does the card say?" Martha asked.

"It says: *'Don't forget me. Heathcliff.'*"

✑ CHAPTER 7 ✑

December 15, 1971

MARTHA WAS WAITING for Winnie to arrive. Winnie had insisted that she do the driving today, and she would help Martha find the perfect gown for the New Year's Eve party as well as one for the tea. She heard a car pull into her driveway so she started to gather her things together for the shopping trip. Just as Winnie opened the front door, Martha's phone rang.

"Hello," Martha said as she motioned for Winnie to come in. "Oh, Lewis, I'm glad you called. Are we still on for the party?"

When Winnie heard this, she headed to the kitchen to give her friend some privacy.

"As you can tell by the schedule I gave you, the party is very long. Some people are arriving the day before and staying at the mansion."

"We don't have to do that, do we?"

"Thank heavens, no. There's going to be an afternoon buffet in the Green Room at 4:30, but we don't have to attend that either. The formal arrival time is not until 7:30, but we must be there ahead of time since Ronald will need my help with some documents before his son and his brother get there. So, my sweet one, I'll pick you up at four."

Just then, she spied Winnie peaking around the doorway. "My friend Winnie is here to go shopping with me. She wants me to look my best for the party."

"Martha, you could put on a burlap bag and you'd still be gorgeous."

"By the way, the roses you sent me for Christmas are still as pretty as the day they were delivered. Thank you so much."

"Unlike Heathcliff, I'll be at your doorstep making sure that no one else takes you to the party. Good-bye, my sweet one."

"Good-bye, Heathcliff." As she hung up the phone, she settled down on the sofa and began hugging the throw pillows.

"Winnie that was Lewis."

"I figured that out all by myself. Now, let's go shopping."

As they drove to the high-end shopping mall, Winnie said, "Since you're going to the mansion for a party and you're going for a tea, you'll soon be packing me in."

"Winnie, don't be foolish. We'll always be friends. I've only been invited—I'm not moving in. For goodness sake. You're my friend. You will always be unless you pack *me* in. Now, look here—Winnie, look at me. We are friends. If I do cultivate a friendship with Mrs. Worthington, she'll never replace you in any way."

"Okay. Let's go shopping," Winnie said as she put on a smile.

"I hear that that new dress shop—the one with the fancy name—has the top of the line when it comes to formal wear. Let's start there."

Before they entered the shop, they looked over the displays in the window. "Oh, these are gorgeous," Martha remarked as she moved slowly down the sidewalk, closely examining each gown. "Some of these expose a lot of skin," Martha said as she laughed.

"This is no time for you to be bashful. You are beautiful and it's time you showed a bit of that to the public," Winnie chided.

In no time at all, a stylist had Martha in the largest dressing area that she had ever seen. A round platform stood in front of a large three-way mirror.

"Miss," the stylist asked, "are you in need of something for a special event?"

"I'm going to a formal New Year's Eve party, so I'll need a gown for that—preferably black. I also have been invited to a tea and I could use some suggestions for that," Martha replied.

"At Bella Luna," Winnie said, glowing with pride.

"Oh, how nice," the stylist replied excitedly. "Did you like any of the styles that are displayed in our window?"

Winnie interrupted, "Not especially. She doesn't want to see herself coming and going at this affair. In other words, she wants a one-of-a-kind."

"I want a long gown. I must be certain that my shoes will not show. You see, I have a slight problem," Martha said, surprising Winnie with this revelation.

"I have a *Nina Forenti* that may just fill all your requirements. As you are probably aware, she makes one copy only of each gown she designs. Let's begin with that," she said to the assistant who immediately left the dressing room.

"Ah, here it is," the stylist said as she carefully took the silk garment bag off the gown. "Isn't this exquisite?"

When she heard the back zipper close, Martha turned slowly to look into the mirror. The stylist was right—it was exquisite. Martha's shoulders were exposed. The form-fitting silk chiffon dress emphasized her tiny waist. A bejeweled pattern of flowers made of crystals and sequins encircled the hips. The style showed off her long, graceful neck. As she stepped back and forth in front of the mirror, the fabric moved as if she had walked into a gentle breeze. She didn't fail to notice that the soft ruffle around the hem completely covered her shoes.

Winnie was all smiles. "Martha, you look super!"

Martha was all smiles, too. "May I ask the price?"

"Remember, it's a *Forenti*." The stylist moved closer to Martha, and said, "It's $4,500."

Martha took a gulp. Winnie was silent.

"I'll take it," Martha said quietly, in a voice she almost didn't recognize.

In no time at all, Martha had also chosen a stunning two-piece silk faille suit with a small peplum in the back in the latest shade of pink. "I'll take this."

As she wrote out the check, Martha said to herself, "Good-bye, new car."

CHAPTER 8

December 25, 1971

IT WAS CHRISTMAS morning and Martha was getting dressed to go to Winnie's house for brunch. For the past three years, ever since Winnie's husband had died, her friend invited *stragglers*, a name Martha gave to the guests who would have had to eat alone on this important day. As she primped before the mirror, Martha was wishing that Lewis would, somehow, be there with her. While realizing that he would be home in two days, she longed for him, so they could sit under the Christmas tree together.

It shocked her when she heard her doorbell chime. Hoping that the wish came true, she hurried to the door. There, to her complete surprise, stood Rocco, the man who had driven her car home from the Holiday Hop.

"Rocco, what a nice surprise," she said as he stood there holding a gift box that had a huge red satin bow on the top.

"Merry Christmas, Miss Harrison. This gift is from Lewis. He told me that he would skin me if I didn't deliver it on Christmas morning," Rocco said as he let out a hearty laugh.

"Merry Christmas, to you, Rocco. Thank you very much. Can I offer you a cup of hot chocolate?"

"No, thanks. I need to hurry home."

Martha sat down on the sofa and held the pretty gift box on her lap. She couldn't imagine what it contained. Slowly, she slid the ribbon off and placed it alongside the throw pillow. When she finally lifted the lid and saw what was inside, the tears began to flow. There, under several layers of tissue paper was an extremely old copy of *Wuthering Heights*. She opened the cover carefully to find it was a first edition copy from the first printing in the States. She knew that the book had first been published in England. Her heart was pounding. "Oh, Lewis, my darling." Wow, she actually said that word.

She thought about the gift she had for Lewis—it was not nearly as romantic or as expensive, as what he had given her. While it too was a book, it was only a silly little thing on how to become a writer. Then, she found a little note, tucked in between the tissue paper. Lewis had written some of the words to *Green Eyes* the song Helen O'Connell of the Tommy Dorsey Band had made so popular, Several lines were underlined: *All through my life they'll taunt me, but will they ever want me, Green eyes, make my dreams come true. What better present can there be but a book for The Book Lady?*

Perhaps she should put this book in a safe deposit box at the bank. It had suffered from the ravages of time and appeared extremely delicate. But, if she did that, she wouldn't be able to hold it any time she wanted. She decided she would ask Lewis for advice.

She curled up on the sofa and looked at the Christmas tree, again. In the low daylight of December, the ornaments glistened and the little lights cast a charm. Even though she was all alone, this Christmas had to be the best one ever. And, in two days, he'd be home.

CHAPTER 9

December 28, 1971

"LEWIS, I HOPE I didn't do something wrong," Martha said as they were driving the twelve miles to Bella Luna.

"Cora just wants to get to meet you before the party. Now, let me tell you about Bella Luna. The property is comprised of 500 acres of woodlands, meadows, trout streams, duck ponds, and waterfalls. One of the most outstanding features is Full Moon Lake, which covers 4 acres. In the center of the lake is a little island with a small Japanese tea house. Maybe this summer we can row a little boat over to the tea house. We can take a basket lunch and a bottle of wine. Maybe we can even take a swim. I think you'll find the island charming. There's also a horse farm, two hunting lodges, a house for the Estate Manager, and several other houses. It's a magnificent place."

"All of that? I can't even imagine a place that wonderful. I hope I'm up to this," Martha said as she checked herself in the mirror on the sun visor.

"Martha, you look beautiful. Cora will love you. Now relax," Lewis said calmly as he took her hand in his. "Think of this visit as a preview for the New Year's Eve party."

Martha watched as the tall, wrought iron gates swung open when Lewis inserted a card into a slot. And, just as quickly, as soon as Lewis' car had passed through, the gates returned to their locked position. A long driveway, lined with trees, led to the front of the mansion. Almost out of nowhere, two men appeared. One of them waved to Lewis, while the other opened the car door for Martha.

On the front of the mansion were stone carvings on either side of the Grand Foyer. There was so much to see and Martha was trying not to miss anything.

"Good afternoon," the butler said as he ushered them into the receiving room where several workers were busily decorating the home for the upcoming party. Employees from a local florist were moving in and around stacks of cartons and piles of live garland as the hallways began to take on a glorious holiday look. Martha noticed how the smell of pine permeated the rooms. "Mrs. Worthington is expecting you," he said to Martha. "Mr. Holmes, Mr. Worthington would like you to meet him in his office." As Lewis walked away, he turned back to Martha and winked. "Follow me please, madam," the butler said as a maid took Martha's cape. "Madam will meet you shortly in the Rose Room."

When Martha stepped into the Rose Room, she wasn't prepared for the sight that was about to entrance her. Her eyes could hardly absorb the beauty and elegance of the room. She realized that she actually was holding her breath. It was, she was convinced, the most beautiful room she had ever seen. No wonder it was called the Rose Room because the entire color scheme was rose and ivory, starting with a thick Aubusson area rug, covering the hardwood floor. As she walked to the center of the room, her eyes were drawn to the lit fireplace that gave not only warmth, but a cheery, inviting aura. Its white marble mantle—Martha was sure it was French—was anchored with two, magnificent Chinese porcelain vases with a pink chrysanthemum motif. However, it was the painting above the fireplace that held Martha spellbound. It was the largest—the most dramatic—painting Martha had ever seen in a private home. A beautiful woman was posed in a sylvan setting. She was dressed in the Roman style and was attended by two white Greyhounds. A hunting bow was in her hand and a quiver of arrows lay at her foot. Among the trees, an alert deer seemed on guard for intruders. Nodding her head, Martha agreed with herself that it was Diana, Goddess of the Hunt. Recalling her knowledge of mythology, she smiled when she remembered that Diana was also the Protectress of the lower classes.

Pulling her attention away from the dominating painting, Martha examined the rest of the room. It was purely feminine. Beautiful Hepplewhite furniture pieces were tastefully placed to create intimate spaces within the room. Martha recognized the style because she had seen pieces at Mr. Nickles' store. It was one of her favorite styles because of the delicate lines. Martha especially loved the embellishments of swags, leaves, and curling ribbons. Fluid and flowing. The style reminded her of ballerinas—maybe Degas dancers—in motion.

As Martha continued her examination of the Rose Room, she noticed that the charm of the room was enhanced by its Christmas décor. The space was teeming with white poinsettias in silver containers. A Christmas tree stood in the corner of the room, laden with silvery snowflakes and sparkling lights. The tree was girded with a rose garland, made from wide, satin ribbon. Topping the tree was an illuminated Waterford finial.

When the door opened, and Cora Worthington stepped in, Martha knew she was about to meet the goddess Diana from the painting. "Miss Harrison, thank you for accepting my invitation. I've been dying to meet you. I must apologize for not giving you proper notice, but I wanted to meet you before the party. You are even more beautiful than Lewis described."

"Thank you, Mrs. Worthington," Martha murmured.

"If you don't mind, I want you to refer to me as Cora. Is it alright with you if I call you Martha?"

"Certainly Mrs. Wor—Cora, this is an absolutely beautiful room. Everything is breathtaking," Martha said nervously.

"I picked the furnishings myself. I didn't need some designer telling me what my side of Bella Luna should look like. And, as usual, Ronnie let me have my way. To celebrate the completion of the room, Ronnie commissioned the painting as a gift. Now, I want to hear about you. Lewis tells me that you're the Director of Public Libraries for Logan County. Just what libraries are in the system?"

"Logan County has four libraries that are now part of one library system. The one in Elmwood Lawn is referred to as the West Branch and specializes in governmental documents and legal books. The East Branch is located in New Springfield and has a marvelous small business section that is the envy of other library systems. Our South Branch has a fine collection of documents on local history. They even provide access to records from several old churches and is located in Sinclair. Oh, those, who are interested in family history and genealogy, love this branch. The North Branch is the one that is the closest to you. It has a delightful children's corner but also has a great collection of classical literature. I hope to take advantage of some of the technologies that are on the horizon to make it easier for clients to get books from any one of the four libraries without having to travel there."

"It sounds as if you have your work cut out for you, But I

can tell that you love your work by the way you talk about your libraries. I have a confession to make. I wanted to meet you because all Lewis wants to discuss lately is you."

Martha was surprised at this statement, but absolutely delighted. Before she was able to respond, there was a gentle knock on the door. "Oh, this must be our tea."

Two servants entered the room to arrange the tea table in front of the fireplace. As they took care of their duties, Cora motioned for Martha to join her on the divan. While they waited, Cora said, "This event is called a "cream tea" because of its intimacy of only two people. Therefore, it is limited to scones and clotted cream and jam. A proper afternoon tea includes a variety of finger sandwiches and desserts. In case you get any invitations for tea, just give me a call and I'll help you unravel some of the complexities involved."

After the servants closed the doors behind them, Cora went on.

"Last week, I had an epiphany. I thought about how I felt the first time I met Ronnie. I had never been around mansions or great wealth, so I was apprehensive when I was exposed to them as a young woman."

"You seem so perfect for this place. It's as if you were born here," Martha said shyly. "By the way, your portrait is stunning."

"I was quite a bit younger, then," Cora said as she laughed. "But I thought I was playing a little joke on Ronnie because I was definitely from the lower classes. When I entered the Grand Foyer so many years ago, three young men were standing there, but only one caught my eye. His smile was warm and my little heart fluttered. Ronnie, his brother Reggie, and their cousin Phillip were having a Kentucky Derby Party and I had been lucky enough to win a contest sponsored by the local radio station—so, there I was. Ronnie approached me and the rest was history. To this day, he still makes me happy whenever I see him."

"How precious. It was meant to happen that way," Martha said as she clapped her hands together. "Sort of like Catherine and Heathcliff."

"Ah, yes. Ronnie and I had to listen while Lewis went on and on about how stupid Heathcliff was because he failed to fight for Catherine. We had so much fun with Lewis that day. One thing that I have learned about Lewis is that he is as honest as the day is long. I have no right to question you about Lewis, but if you believe that he's the one, go for it. If you two develop a relationship, don't forget the little things. My husband's office faces the east. Each morning, he gets up, takes a seat on the divan near the huge window and watches the sunrise. Every once in a while," Cora paused for a moment and Martha had a sense that she was enjoying a precious memory, "I show up with a tray of cinnamon rolls and coffee. We sit, side by side, watching the world wake up. Occasionally, I slip little notes into his dressing robe pocket, or the suit he has hanging out to wear the next day, that have a few words of love. Love is like a plant—it must be cultivated. At one time, Ronnie traveled a great deal. Now, that he has Lewis by his side, he seldom leaves our home."

"Cora, thank you for sharing that with me. My childhood was not the greatest and I sometimes have a difficult time believing that I am worthy of anything. You see, I was born on Pearl Harbor Day..."

Cora moved over and wrapped her arms around Martha. "Oh, Martha, that was not your fault. You're a, well-educated woman, who has the stamina and willpower to make her own way. You have to know that Lewis is in love with you. If you feel the same way, let him know. Remember, we each have a given amount of time with one another. We can't afford to waste it. Don't let that happen to you. Use your time well."

↝ CHAPTER 10 ↜

December 31, 1971

I T WAS NEW Year's Eve day and Martha was watching the clock. She swore that it hadn't moved for hours. But tonight could change her life. All she could think about was Lewis and how it had felt, when he had held her in his arms while dancing at the Holiday Hop. Perhaps it was way too soon for her to feel this way about a man she barely knew. There had been only one other man—and that was long ago—who had excited her, but she had never acted on that feeling. She laughed when she realized that people could call her an *old maid*.

She never would have dreamed that so many wonderful things could have happened to make her life so different. First, and most importantly, Lewis loved her. Then, there was that wonderful day when she had met Cora Worthington. And, spending so much for a dress was out of character. She told herself that she really didn't need a new car—but, then again, she might wear the dress just one time.

Taking her dress out of the garment bag, she hung it over the closet door. She loved touching it. Feeling the silk under her fingers gave her comfort. She made a vow that she would no longer worry about spending so much money. Her vow was interrupted when Winnie arrived with her arms filled with the tools she needed to do Martha's hair. "My goodness, Winnie, it looks as if you're moving in," Martha chuckled as Winnie swung into action.

They discussed at length the styles that would be suitable for Martha's face, the occasion, and the dress. Martha had objected when Winnie proposed a low chignon with soft, loose French braids on the sides. "I don't want to look like a librarian with a knot."

Winnie said, "Trust me. I will make you look like Princess Grace at a Monte Carlo gala. Your hair is so thick and silky that you'll look elegant and womanly."

Martha relaxed and trusted her best friend to work magic. She watched in amazement as Winnie twisted and twirled strings of pearls in and out of the curls and braids. When Winnie was finished—and allowed Martha a long look in the mirror—both women were astonished with the results.

"Martha, you look so refined and classy."

"Now, let's get you dressed so that I can get out of here before Prince Charming arrives," Winnie said as she lifted the dress off the hanger.

"Wait, Winnie, wait. I just remembered Elizabeth's sash," she said excitedly as she quickly got the box and showed Winnie a beaded purse and a black satin sash with tiny pearl fringes at the ends.

"God, they're precious. You're one lucky lady," Winnie said as she fingered all the sashes that were neatly folded and nestled in tissue paper. "Wait, Martha. Use the purse, but not the sash. It will hide some of the most beautiful beaded work on the dress. Save the sash for another event."

"Martha, you look so exceptional."

"Do I look as if I really belong at Bella Luna?"

"Belong! Hell, you look as if you own it," Winnie said as she kissed Martha on the cheek. "Bye, my little friend. Happy New Year," Winnie said as she rushed out the door.

After Winnie had left, Martha stood in front of the floor-length mirror for many minutes. Years ago, she had stopped looking at herself with a critical eye. Actually, she had stopped looking at herself in any exacting way. But now, she examined her image with a long stare. She wasn't sure what she was seeing. Was it really her? It must be the dress... or the hair style. Yes. It was both of these things, and, yet, it was something more. Martha had never seen herself look so grand. She *felt* beautiful, but she knew better. She only hoped that this "look" would help her fit in tonight and prayed that Lewis would find her appealing.

She jumped when the doorbell rang. Opening the door, she smiled and said, "Good evening, sir, may I help you?"

Lewis stood there for a moment, allowing himself time to look at Martha. "My God, you are a vision."

"Thank you, sir," she replied.

"Martha, you look fabulous," he uttered as he stepped into the living room. "I'm not sure that I should take you to the party. You look so beautiful others may steal you away," Lewis said as he helped Martha put on her cape.

It was difficult for Lewis to drive. All he wanted to do was look at her. "You know, you're going to be envied by every woman at this party."

As they pulled into the driveway at Bella Luna, a young man approached and opened the car door. "Good evening, Miss. Good evening, Sir." Then, he quickly whisked the car away.

When they stepped into the Grand Foyer, Martha was

taken aback with the cavernous size and the sheer beauty of the sight that glistened brightly under a row of crystal chandeliers. It was even more glorious than when she had come here to see Cora. She had done a bit of research on Bella Luna to get a feeling for how this magnificent building had come to be. She learned that much of the work had been done by immigrants, who brought their skills with them from Europe. Among the workers were stone masons, stone carvers, carpenters, and metal workers—the same workers who had built many of the churches in the area. Ronald's grandfather had been recommended to the Vanderbilts and were rapidly accepted by the so-called inner-circle. Now, Martha stood there, surrounded by things that screamed wealth, holding on to Lewis's hand, amazed and terrified. The thought that she would be socializing with financiers, artists, businessmen, industrialists, social VIPs, European nobility and even theater types was beyond her comprehension.

"Here comes my boss," whispered Lewis.

"Oh, Lewis, thank you so much for bringing the documents. I apologize for this, but you and I must review them before my brother and my son get here."

"Ronald, this beautiful lady is Martha Harrison. She's the Director of Public Libraries for our county."

"My Cora can't stop talking about you. I apologize for having to take Lewis away for a bit. I'll try not to keep him too long," Mr. Worthington said as he held Martha's hand.

Martha was ushered into the Morning Room to wait. She noticed a painting hanging over the fireplace and was certain that it was a Renoir. Before too long, Lewis appeared and said, "You look perfect in this type of setting. Ronald suggested that I give you a tour. Or, it's time for cocktails and hors d'oeuvres, if you would like. Which do you prefer?"

"Oh, Lewis, I would love to see the rest of Bella Luna."

Martha was aware of the aroma of flowers everywhere. She wondered what the florist's bill must be. She had never seen so many flowers in one place and wanted to take it all in so that she could remember this night forever. Everywhere they walked, there seemed to be fireplaces that were adorned with garlands, silver bells, and tiny white lights.

"Lewis, it must take a huge staff to take care of this magnificent structure."

"I don't know the exact number, but whenever there's a party, it could probably go as high as seventy people," Lewis said as they headed back to the Grand Foyer. As Lewis guided her towards the dining room, where the Worthingtons were "receiving," he whispered, "He told me that his wife adores you."

Ronald Worthington stepped forward, "Hello again," he said to Martha. I don't know why such a classy lady is bothering with a reprobate like you."

"Martha, don't pay any attention to what my husband says. I'm delighted to see both of you again. As is our custom, we seat our guests randomly around the dinner table so that they can get to know one another. However, we've seated Lewis to your right, and Reggie, Ronnie's brother, to your left. He's a little different, but lots of fun."

"By the way, Lewis, you did a nice job with Andrews. In fact, it was more than I had expected," Ronald said.

"Now, Ronnie, you promised—no business tonight," Cora reminded her husband.

"You see, Miss Harrison, I may be an astute investor, but Cora still rules the roost," Ronald said as he patted Lewis on his back. "Myrtle will show you to your seats. Miss Harrison, save me a dance, please."

"Ronnie, one of these days you may be shot by a jealous husband," Cora said as she smiled adoringly at her husband.

As they stepped into the dining room, Martha thought she had now entered fairyland. Tables, dressed in white linen cloths with extra-large monogrammed napkins, provided the background for the sterling silver monogrammed silverware. Limoges china settings, decorated with delicate pink almond flowers, lily of the valley, and miniature rose-colored carnations, with silver chargers, finished each setting. Cut glass Baccarat stemware glistened under the light generated by enormous 12-armed candelabra placed every five feet down the tables set for 120 guests. Interspersed, were tall Waterford crystal vases, teaming with white roses, pink Asiatic lilies, chrysanthemums, and thin, white-painted branches that were laden with hundreds of glass "grapes".

As Martha took her seat, Mr. Worthington took the mic exactly at 9 o'clock. "My friends, here we are once again gathered to usher in a fresh, new year. We have high hopes that the New Year will bring us health and happiness. We take with us memories of 1971, some good, some not so good. Let's nurture what is the most important element in our lives—our families and friends. Raise your glasses high and drink a toast to one another."

"Here...here..." the guests cheered and applauded their host.

As Martha was shaking Reggie Worthington's hand, her voice was extremely weak. She was pleased that Reggie seemed quite content carrying on most of the conversation.

"Miss Harrison, I don't mean to pry into your life, but I simply can't believe that someone as beautiful as you is a librarian," Reggie said.

Lewis leaned forward. He wanted to make sure that Reggie

was not saying anything inappropriate to Martha. He never trusted Ronald's brother, and he had had suspicions about the guy, who seemed to move in and out of Ronald's life on a whim.

"I fell in love with libraries and books when I was a young child. And, becoming a librarian was my dream job," Martha said proudly.

"Then, you are to be congratulated. Most of us never find that dream job. Ronnie found his—he makes money in order to make more money," Reggie said with a hearty laugh. "My family is still waiting for me to find a career."

"Mr. Worthington…"

"*Reggie*, please. I only come to these things to get my brother off my back. He can't believe that I'm not interested in making money. My father gave me plenty of that, but what he didn't give me was a desire to do anything. In fact, he would repeatedly tell me that I couldn't do anything, so I took him at his word." He let out another roar of laughter. "Now, we have to get ready for what always seems to be a hundred courses. We get a little of this and a little of that. For God's sake, we just had tons of hors d'oeuvres. To be honest with you, dear Martha, I'd rather have a cheeseburger from McDonald's."

"Oh, this looks scrumptious," Martha said as the waiter served the first course.

The waiter, who was obviously captivated with Martha, whispered, "Anjou pear salad with goat cheese, fennel black walnuts and white balsamic."

"Now, we must wait forever to get the next course. Oops, here it comes already. This is more to my liking: poached Maine lobster with carrots and mushrooms. Of course, the portions are large enough to feed a baby bird," Reggie said as he laughed again.

"Lemon sorbet," Martha said as the waiter slid a small sterling silver dish in front of her.

"You know what that means when they serve the sorbet?"

"And, what does that mean?" Martha asked as she smiled at Reggie.

"It's almost time for the real stuff," Reggie responded.

As they worked their way through the courses, none of the guests were aware that two men were hiding in the shrubbery that formed a semi-circle around the large, brick patio.

"Hell, Mookey, these cats are still eating. Don't they ever get done?"

"I figure they've got an hour to go before the dancing begins. Do you see the bling that these babes have on? Any other time some of that bling would be just fine for me, but I have work to do tonight."

"Mookey, how in hell did you find a way into this damned fortress?"

"Well, I knew they had to have a way for delivery trucks to get into and out of this joint. Luckily, it's right near the lake. I also discovered a large shed where they keep the boats. The roof of that shed is just low enough for me to hoist myself up to the top of the wall. And, inside that shed, I found a spare key, so I had a copy made. Can you imagine that? They won't be able to figure out how anyone got in. See, that's why Mack pays me more than he pays you."

"You sure are smart," Fat Tony said sadly.

"The rifle comes out tonight. I don't know why he just didn't want me to shoot the bastard. No, instead he wants me to wing him. Do you realize how hard that's gonna be in a crowd like this. Maybe I'll just have to shoot in the air."

"Mookey, I don't want no part of killing—I told you that before. Just shoot in the air and that should scare the hell out of them."

"We'll see—we'll see."

CHAPTER 11

December 31, 1971

LEWIS WAS CONCERNED that Reggie might be annoying Martha. But when he watched her, he could tell that she was having a good time. She smiled often and winked at Lewis several times.

"Now, this is what I call food," Reggie said as the waiter served rib eye with crisp onions, double stuffed potatoes, and creamed spinach. Reggie was quiet for a short period of time and then said, "Here comes Chateau Mouton Rothschild. Waiter, let me see the label. Oh, 1955. Very nice."

Martha couldn't help herself. "Reggie, you're a hoot."

"Well, I figured you'd need something on the light side. You know, financial hound dogs, like Lewis, get excited only when they talk about money. Isn't that right, Lewis?"

"You're so right, Reggie. I'm happy that you like Martha."

"Hells, bells, Lewis, look at her—beautiful, charming, and she's not a stuffed shirt like some people I know," Reggie said as he dug into the dessert: nectarine tart with crème Fraiche ice cream. "One more thing to go, Martha, and that will be Schramsberg Cremant, 1914. Ronnie always ends these things with his favorite."

When Ronald stood up, everyone stopped talking. "I'd like

to invite all our ladies to the Palm Room for coffee. Cora is looking forward to showing off her orchids and bougainvillea. Gentlemen, please join me in the library for brandy. At midnight, we'll usher in the New Year with a champagne toast on the enclosed balcony. As a special treat, we have invited Scottish pipers to play *Auld Lang Syne.*

During the time when the men and women were separated, the waiters were lining up silver trays with Waterford flutes for the toast. Five Scottish pipers marched in and took their places at the far end of the balcony. When the guests entered the patio, they were thrilled to see the pipers in their regalia. They watched closely as little boats moved around the lake to get into position for the fireworks, provided by the famous Bonatti Brothers. Reggie, holding a kettle drum, shouted, "Here we go, folks—the midnight countdown to a new year." As he counted, the guests joined in. When they shouted "one", and yelled "Happy New Year!" As a flurry of fireworks was set off from the boats on Full Moon Lake. Guests raised their glasses and lots of hugs and kisses were exchanged. When the Scottish pipers played, everyone sang along.

Mookey, sprawled out on the roof of the boat house, holding a rifle with a long-range scope, took aim at his target. Suddenly, snow from the tree branch above his head, broke free. Mookey shuddered when the snow hit his head, and without meaning to do it, he pulled the trigger. He let loose with a barrage of curses when he realized that he had dropped the rifle and it had fallen into thick greenery below. Sliding down the outside of the wall, Mookey was relieved to see that Fat Tony was sitting in their car with the motor running and the door opened. He motioned for Fat Tony to wait as he rummaged through his pockets and pulled out a large key which he used to open the gate. It didn't take him long to find his rifle. He hustled out the gate and fell into the car.

"Did you scare them?" Fat Tony asked anxiously as he pulled out.

"How the hell would I know? The damned snow made me pull the trigger—maybe I did—maybe I didn't. Holy hell. What a mess," Mookey said as he wiped the water off his head. "We'll know in the morning. If I hit him, it'll be big news."

As Fat Tony drove the car away, the pipers were still playing and the guests were singing loudly. He knew better than to ask Mookey how he was gonna explain what happened tonight to the big boss. Fat Tony smiled. The boss wouldn't think Mookey was so smart anymore.

⊰⊱ CHAPTER 12 ⊰⊱

January 1, 1972

A S SOON AS the fireworks ended, the guests began ambling to the ballroom. The crystal chandeliers created a heavenly aura as they reflected all the sparkling lights that were on gold-tinted evergreens that lined the walls. Small sterling silver bowls, filled with white berries and Christmas greens were on tables that encircled the beautiful parquet floor. To begin the dancing, Cora and Ronald moved hand-in-hand, to the center of the ballroom. Ronald gently took her in his arms as the orchestra played *Stardust*. The guests applauded politely. Cora was radiant as she smiled up at her husband. Martha, who was holding Lewis' hand, realized that she was observing a couple, who, even after thirty years of marriage, was still in love. That kind of love—that's what Martha wanted.

Very shortly, the ballroom was a sight to behold. The ladies were dressed to the nines and the gentlemen looked superb in their tuxedos as they twirled their partners to the tempo of the music. After the couples had had an opportunity to dance several sets, the trumpet player approached the mic. "Ladies and gentlemen, I've received a request, but I want to tell you a bit about why I really love to do this particular song. This past July we lost *Sachmo*—Louis Armstrong—the

DORIS M. DORWART, Ed.D.

golden trumpeter. While he grew up in a home for waifs and strays, he found the trumpet and we were blessed. He is given credit for making *Hello, Dolly* the number one hit of 1964. So, if you'd like to sing along, please do so." Soon the words to *Hello, Dolly* were reverberating throughout the ballroom. At the same time, multi-colored streamers and balloons floated down from the ceiling. Suddenly, a loud crack of thunder, followed by a vivid streak of lightning, startled the guests. Then, it started to rain extremely hard.

"Well," Reggie said as he spoke into the mic. "With that clap of thunder, it appears that Mother Nature is trying to outdo us with noise to bring in the New Year. So, let's do the countdown again and see if we can beat Mother Nature at her own game. Our drummer will help us to count 10 to 1—here we go!" The guests joined in by counting as the drummer banged his drum as loudly as possible. Covered with streamers and popping balloons, clearly they were enjoying bringing in the New Year once again. Reggie was pleased that the guests participated and even renewed the kissing and hugging.

While Reggie was trying to find Martha, Lewis had managed to get her off to the side of the room where they could be alone. He slid his arm around her and pulled her tightly to his chest. She tilted her head back, placed her hand on the back of his neck, and kissed him passionately. They stood that way for a while, finally breaking apart and smiling broadly at one another.

"Happy New Year, my beautiful Green Eyes."

"Happy New Year, Heathcliff."

The moment was interrupted when Reggie found Martha. "Martha, may I have the next dance? I see this young fellow is monopolizing you, so I have come to your rescue," Reggie said playfully and bowed dramatically.

"Certainly," Martha replied as she winked at Lewis.

Lewis immediately went to Cora's table and asked her for a dance. Cora said, "Lewis, dance over to where Martha and Reggie are and cut-in on him. She's probably had enough of his silliness."

As they closed in on Reggie, Cora laughed since she knew what was coming next. Lewis tapped Reggie on the shoulder, "Excuse me, sir, but I'm cutting-in."

Before he truly knew what had happened, Reggie found himself dancing with his sister-in-law. "What happened?" he asked Cora.

"It's called young love, Reggie. Isn't it wonderful to watch? Now, all they have to do is keep it alive," Cora stated.

Lewis maneuvered Martha over to the doorway. "There will be another meal served in a bit. But, if you'd like to leave now, we can quietly thank our hosts and slip out the doorway."

"You read my mind," she said as she squeezed his hand.

As they thanked their hosts, Cora said, "Lewis, Jennifer is at the cloak room with the gift bags. Make sure you each get one," she said as she kissed Lewis on his cheek.

Moments later, Lewis and Martha were driving away. "You may want to look in that bag," Lewis said as he maneuvered a curve.

Martha turned the overhead light on. "Oh, Lewis, look. A Tiffany silver bracelet with 1972 on a charm. Oh, my. There are also two DeLaffee's Grand Cru Chocolate Truffles in a silk-covered wooden gift box. I've heard about these, but I never thought I would actually see one. I wonder if the same thing is in your bag."

"Only the ladies received the chocolates. The men were given a silver paperweight, engraved with 1972 in a Tiffany box. Ronnie asked me for my opinion on the gifts some time ago. I'm surprised I didn't blurt this out or I would have spoiled the party favor."

As they drove to Martha's home, they were both silent. With her head on Lewis's shoulder and clasping his hand, she was lost in the blissfulness of the moment.

When they arrived at Martha's home, she said, "Lewis, I never had an opportunity to give you your Christmas gift. Let's sit by the tree. Remarkably, your gift is something like the one you gave me—only less expensive."

As they sat side by side, Martha handed Lewis his gift. When he saw the title of the book—*How to Become a Writer*—he broke out in laughter. "That's from the diner—Martha, you are amazing. If the book makes me a writer, I'll tell the world how wonderful you are, but I'm not sure that any words can convey to you how much you mean to me."

"The world could stop revolving right now, Lewis. I have never been this happy. I owe this all to you."

Lewis took Martha's hand and said, "Martha, you probably know by now how crazy I am about you. While I'm ready to take our relationship to the next level, I want to leave the timing up to you."

"How sweet of you, Lewis."

"When you're ready just say *'I'm ready'*."

"I'm ready?" Martha asked.

"Yes."

"Lewis, I'm ready," she said as she stood up.

Lewis sat still for a moment. "You—you mean it?"

"Yes, my darling."

Lewis jumped up. "Wait here. Don't move. I'll be right back."

Martha heard the sound of a trunk lid being slammed

shut. Lewis popped back in, holding a duffel bag. "Sweetheart, I put this in the trunk with high hopes."

Martha moved towards him. Lewis dropped the bag. They embraced.

"Martha, my Martha, I love you so much."

"Lewis, will you please turn the tree lights off?" Martha asked as she headed up the stairs. Her heart was beating so fast she thought that it might jump out of her body.

As they entered her bedroom, Martha said, "You can put your things on the chaise lounge. I'll see you in a few minutes."

Lewis watched as she disappeared into the bathroom. He undressed quickly and got under the covers. Suddenly, she stood in front of him. "Lewis, I have something to tell you."

"Please don't tell me that you have fallen in love with Reggie," Lewis said, trying to cut the tension to a manageable level.

She laughed as she dropped her bathrobe and quickly slid into the bed beside him. Lewis sighed and held his breath. As she slipped her arm around his broad, bare chest, she snuggled up to him and gently whispered into his ear, "Lewis, I want you to know that this will be a first for me. Please be patient."

From there on, there was no need for words. Apparently, the moon, the stars, and the earth were all aligned.

CHAPTER 13

January 1, 1972

LEWIS WOKE UP to the smell of coffee. He reached across the bed. Slowly, he rolled around and grabbed the pillow where Martha had lain her head last night—or was it early this morning. He had never felt so relaxed and content as he did at this moment. Glancing at the little clock beside Martha's bed, he saw that it was ten—way past the time he usually started his day. He finally got into a sitting position and began to examine Martha's bedroom. Somehow, the room seemed serene and comfortable—beautiful, just like Martha. As he stood up, he got a closer look at her vanity table. There, nestled between two sets of drawers, was an old-fashioned monogrammed set of brushes and jars—each bearing the letter *"E"*. Then, he spotted a white lace glove protruding out of one of the drawers. He smiled. The room could only belong to one woman—his woman.

When he flicked the light on in the bathroom, he saw that she had written him a note on the mirror with her lipstick. *Sweetie, when you're ready, come downstairs for breakfast.*

He took a shower and dressed as quickly as he could. Clutching his shoes and socks in his hands, he ran down the steps and into the living room. As he sat down on a winged-back chair, he called out, "Hey beautiful, I'm here."

"Good morning, Lewis," she responded.

As Lewis leaned down to tie his shoes, his eyes landed on a framed photograph that was resting on an end table. He didn't believe what he saw. "What the hell?" He got up and grabbed the picture and examined it closely. "Martha, how do you know Howard McKnight?"

"Who?"

"Howard McKnight. I used to call him *bucky beaver*. His photograph is sitting on your end table," Lewis answered, as unpleasant thoughts began to run through his brain.

Martha, wearing a short terry cloth bathrobe, came into the living room. "Oh, there's a story to that. I'm addicted to buying vintage things, especially at Nickles. The other week, I found an album that was filled with photos obviously taken by professional photographers. Many of them were signed *To Dorothy*. I was shocked when I learned that she was the girl who was murdered some time ago. I cringed when Nickles told me that her body had been stuffed into a suitcase. I felt so sorry for the woman that I thought, if I bought the album, I'd be able to protect it from any additional harm. Does that sound rationale?"

"So, McKnight's photograph was in the album?"

"Yes. I wanted to use the frame I bought and I couldn't find an appropriate photograph to use, so I looked in the album. He looked like a nice person, and his picture fit into the frame perfectly. Lewis, you seem perturbed. What's wrong? Why did you call him *bucky beaver*?"

Lewis didn't answer immediately. He held the picture frame in his hands while staring at the floor. "I used to be a bully, Martha, That is until Ronald found out and made me stop. Martha, do you still have the album?"

"Sure," she said as she walked over to the bookshelf and pulled it from the bottom shelf.

Lewis flipped it open. "Martha, these are all actors who sometimes appeared in summer stock. I met McKnight when I was a cub reporter for the town newspaper. He was personable and I thought he was an important star. At first we got along fine. He invited me to attend a party and that's when I met several other actors."

"What about Dorothy? Where does she fit in?"

"She was the secretary for the man who booked actors—Jim something— can't remember his last name," Lewis said as he continued to flip through the pages. "Good God, here's Rosa."

"Maybe I shouldn't ask, but who was she?"

"Rosa Gonzales. At one time, she was dating Howard. That was until he caught Rosa and me in a necking session at a party," Lewis said as he laughed.

A little pang of jealousy hit Martha. "Did you two have a fight over her?"

"Heavens, no. Although that did end the friendship between Howard and me. Rosa went her own way after that and I don't know what happened to her. However, Howard always had had his heart set on becoming a famous actor. While that never happened, I do know that he's now working as a movie director. With such a rich father, Howard can probably buy his way in anywhere."

"Perhaps I should discard the album," Martha suggested, all the while planning on at least tossing Rosa's picture in the trash.

"Doesn't that album give you the creeps?" Lewis asked.

"It's beginning to. I just thought it would be nice to take care of it for her—or is that creepy?"

"You know, I just got an idea. Perhaps you should turn the album over to the police. I've heard that the new DA is going to re-open the case. Maybe, just maybe, these pictures might aid them in their investigation. I realize that she knew a lot of people, but perhaps Dorothy's killer is in the album. If you'd prefer, I could take care of that for you. It's a holiday, so the DA probably won't be in his office. I tell you what: I can take it to him on Friday when I get back from my next trip."

"Lewis, how did you get from being a party-goer with the actors, to working for the Worthingtons?"

"My mother and Cora Worthington are sisters. So, I had easy access to both Ronald and Cora. It was Ronald who got me to settle down and grow up. He's one of the kindest, most patient men I have ever met. It took me awhile to understand life in general, but I loved being his "wing man" and sniffing out the right firms. There were times that both Matthew, Ronald's son, and I worked the same case. Matthew was a much faster learner than I was and he was quickly made head of the Zurich branch. Fortunately, I developed a bond with Ronald and I honestly believe that he looks at me as a son. Now, I do believe that I smell coffee, you sweet thing," he said as he swept Martha into his arms and they kissed. "That's our first kiss for 1972. I must tell you, I'm planning on getting at least 50 per day."

"If memory serves me correctly, you got more than that just a few hours ago."

"Well, if memory serves me correctly, you're right. Martha," he said softly as he put his hand under her chin and raised her head a bit, "you're what I've been searching for. When I told you last night that I loved you, you put your hand over my lips. I don't expect you to say the same thing to me right now, but I'm willing to wait to hear those words."

"You know, Lewis, Rosa has no idea what she missed!"

The two lovers sat side by side, eating toasted bagels and drinking coffee, all the while taking time out for more kissing. When Martha got up and sat on Lewis's lap, he put his hands on the sash of her bathrobe and teased, "I wonder what would happen if I pulled on this?"

"Why don't you do that—then we'll both know what will happen."

Just as Lewis reached for Martha, the phone rang. She leaned over his body and grabbed the phone. "Hello," she laughed as she saw the disappointment on Lewis' face. "Certainly, Mr. Worthington. He's right here," Martha said as she handed him the phone.

"Happy New Year, Ronald," Lewis said. "Something wrong?"

"Do you by any chance remember hearing a rifle shot last night?"

"What? A rifle shot? No, why?"

"Well," Ronald said, "The groundskeeper stopped by to report that he found a shell casing near the boat house. Of course, with the heavy rain we had later, it could have been there for some time. But, I called to have the locks changed on the rear gate and the boat house, just in case."

"Smart move. Everyone was having such a good time and the fireworks were the best ever. S, if there was someone there with a rifle, and they shot it off, as far as we know no one was hurt. It wouldn't hurt, however, to call Chief Weaver and share this information with him."

"Okay, Lewis. Oh, I apologize for calling you at Martha's home. Cora wanted me to wait until tomorrow, but you know me. Sorry," Ronald chuckled. "You may not know this, but I was young at one time, too. Happy New Year!"

CHAPTER 14

February 9, 1972

MARTHA AND WINNIE had managed to get their favorite table at Alberto's Steak House even though it was a Wednesday night, or *Music Night*, as it was advertised, so it had become the busiest night of the week for the well-known restaurant. The table was close enough to the small stage so that they could enjoy the music, but not too close that they couldn't hold a conversation.

"How come you're not with Lewis tonight?" Winnie asked in an irritated voice as she perused the menu that she already knew by heart.

"He's on another business trip for Worthington. He'll be home on Friday. I'm sorry if you feel that I'm ignoring you," Martha said trying to soothe her dearest friend," she said as she smiled.

"Oh, I know, Martha. I can't say that I blame you, but I've been spoiled for so long that it'll take me some time to learn to share you with him."

"What looks good to you?" Martha asked as she watched Winnie closely.

"I think I'll get the petite steak. You can't go wrong with that," Winnie said.

"Winnie, I have a question to ask you, and I want you to be honest with me. This is the first time in my life that I've experienced the kind of love that I feel for Lewis. He already has told me that he loves me. I haven't said that to him. He's also told me that he's willing to wait to hear those words. Now, for the question—is it too early for either of us to talk about love?"

"Martha, you two are adults—not kids, who have no idea what love really is. And, if you want to have children, may I remind you that your biological clock is ticking," Winnie said softly.

Martha blushed. "I never thought about that."

"Whether or not you want kids, I would encourage you to open your heart and let love walk in. Martha, you're entitled to grab your happiness. Every time you talk about him, you glow. Run with it, my friend. If it was meant to be, you'll be rewarded many times over. Don't be afraid. I know what that feeling is. I never regretted the time I spent with Brian. And, the three years I had him before that damned accident were the best I ever had."

"Winnie, you're so special to me."

After the waiter took their order, Winnie asked, "Where's Lewis this time?"

"Would you believe New York City?" Martha replied.

"That's not an exotic place, but I guess a lot of financial transactions occur there. Listen to me, like I know what's happening in the world of finances. I should know just a tiny bit what Worthington knows and then I might be wealthy, too. Where does Lewis stand as far as the Worthingtons are concerned?"

"I just learned that Cora Worthington is his aunt. He loves

both Cora and Ronald. I know a little bit about Lewis' job. Should I ask more questions?"

"Only you can decide that, Martha. Sometimes it's better not to know."

"Oh, by the way, I got a call from Nickles. He said some man was in his shop and asked to see the things from the Evans' estate—you know, the woman in the suitcase. Well, anyway, the guy specifically asked about a photograph album. He claimed that he knew Dorothy and was looking for a keepsake. Fortunately, Mr. Nickles said he didn't remember who bought it."

"Martha, I think you should toss that album. I get the shivers when I just think about it."

"I feel sorry for Dorothy. So, the least I can do is save it for her. I put it in the bottom drawer of the desk in my den. It will be safe there."

As the two friends enjoyed their dinner and glasses of merlot, they were unaware that Mookey and Fat Tony were cruising the parking lot of the restaurant.

"That's her car over there. Good, it's not under a light," Fat Tony said. "This will be easy."

"I don't know why Mack wants us to slash her tires. I thought he'd want to hurt her, but he says not to touch her. He wants to get some fun out of this one. He seems to change his damned mind every time I turn around," Mookey said angrily. "Just as long as he keeps the money flowing our way, I'll do what he asks. He's the boss, so let's do it and get the hell out of here."

CHAPTER 15

February 10, 1972

"ALL FOUR TIRES?" Lewis asked as he looked at Martha with concern.

"Yes. Some men from the restaurant came to our rescue. Lewis, I can't figure out why someone would do that to my car."

Lewis thought for a few moments. "Was anyone jealous that you received your promotion?"

"Heavens, I don't think so. But someone must be very angry with me," Martha said as she took Lewis' hand.

"Were the police called?"

"Yes," Martha responded, surprised at the anger she heard in Lewis' voice.

Lewis tried to push thoughts away that someone might be stalking him and was now including Martha in on that hatred. Or, it might be that he had stepped on toes in some of the deals that he had arranged for Worthington. After all, the finance world could be as cutthroat as politics. He had always managed to know his competition and, consequently, had avoided the slimier crowd of his business. When he was forced to deal with a vile element, he knew how to watch his back. But, now, his heart sank. He loved Martha with every fiber of his being and he may now have put her in danger. He needed to protect her without frightening her.

"Just to be safe, I'm going to order a bodyguard for you."

"Do you really think that's necessary? It just might have been some kids out causing trouble," Martha suggested.

"To be safe, I want to protect you. If nothing further happens, we can call the bodyguard off. Meanwhile, you won't be aware most of the time that anyone is guarding you. My guys are good. More importantly, you, my darling, will be safe. You'll be able to go about your normal routines; he won't get in your way. However, I did make an appointment with Chief Weaver for Monday. Would you like to go along?"

"I have to go to the South Branch Library to read to the children. I'll get the album for you," Martha said as she headed to her den. Suddenly, she called out sharply, "Lewis, come here."

Lewis, sensing some urgency, hurried into the den. "What's wrong?"

"The album. It's gone."

"Are you certain that you didn't move it?"

"I put it in the bottom drawer of my desk and locked it just to keep it safe. Who could have taken it?" Martha said on the verge of tears.

"Has anyone been in your home lately?"

"Well, my neighbor was here yesterday and Winnie was here last night. Oh, I forgot, I did get a strange call from Mr. Nickles. He told me that a man had come into his shop and inquired about items from Dorothy Evans' estate and that he also mentioned the album."

"Martha, you mean to tell me that something this important happened and you simply forgot to tell me?" Lewis said without bothering to cover up his frustration. "I called you twice while I was in New York. Why didn't you tell me then?"

"I didn't want to bother you and—"

"When it comes to your safety, it's not a bother. What else has happened that you haven't told me?" Lewis said angrily.

"Mr. Nickles told the man that someone had already purchased the album, but he didn't tell him who. He even offered Mr. Nickles money if he could recall the name of the person who bought it."

"How can I protect you when you do something like this? I can't do that without knowing everything that happens to that damned album. From now on, I expect that you'll keep me posted on anything that happens regarding the album or Dorothy Evans."

Martha was quiet. This was a side of Lewis that she hadn't seen before, and she wasn't sure how to handle it. "I'm so sorry, Lewis. You know, Lewis, you were probably right about the album—a photograph of Dorothy's killer had to be in there."

"What about McKnight's photo? What did you do with that?"

"Before I put the album away, I put his photo back in its original place. Why do you ask?" Martha said quietly, trying hard not to cry.

"Someone wants that album. I'm certain that there are copies of many of the photos Dorothy had in there. So, if it wasn't the picture they're after, it could be that Dorothy had written something on the back of one of them—something that they do not want anyone else to know. The best strategy now is not to tell the police that the album is missing. If we act like we feel that the album is still in the desk drawer, they might leave you alone."

"I'm truly sorry, Lewis," Martha said as he hurried out the door. "I didn't know."

Over his shoulder, he said, "Well, now you do."

Martha fell to her knees. When she heard the door slam, she began to weep. Her body was racked with pain as real as any she had ever known. She was sobbing so hard that she almost couldn't breathe. Suddenly, she felt two arms encircling her. He had returned. "My darling, my darling, please forgive me. I'm such an ass. I only want to protect you—I don't want to hurt you and look what I did. Sweetheart, please, please forgive me," Lewis said as he cradled her in his arms. "I don't deserve your forgiveness. I promise I'll never hurt you like that again."

CHAPTER 16

February 11, 1972

M ARTHA HAD JUST entered her office at the Logan County Courthouse when her phone rang.

"Miss Harrison. How may I help you?"

"Martha, Martha," Gwen Preston, Director of the North Branch Public Library, said through her tears. "Martha, someone destroyed our little Story Land Corner. Oh, Martha, you must come, hurry."

"Gwen, did you call the police?"

"No, should I?" Gwen asked.

"Yes. Call them immediately. Close the library. Put a sign on the front door that your facility is temporarily closed. We don't want anyone to be walking around the crime area. Don't touch or move anything. Pull yourself together, Gwen. We'll make things right again. I'll see you shortly."

Martha grabbed her notebook and a camera. On her way, she realized that Lewis had been right to be concerned. Why else would anyone want to destroy an area that was designed for toddlers to enjoy picture books, while sitting in pretty wooden white swans? Since it had been three weeks when nothing went wrong, Martha had hoped that the problems were over.

As she ran up the steps to enter the library, she was pleased to see that Gwen had placed a sign on the door. She also noted that a police car was parked at the curb. When she got a good look at the damage that was done to the Story Land Corner, she was devastated. The swans were in pieces, book covers were ripped off many of the books, and the little animal figures that were hiding behind little cardboard trees were ripped to shreds.

When she heard Lewis' voice, she quickly spun around. "Lewis, how did you find out about this?" she said, as she pointed to the destruction.

"Rocco called me," he replied as he stepped forward and took her hand. "This was planned to hurt you, Martha. Now, what we must do is find out who has such a grudge against you that they would stoop this low."

"Rocco? I never saw him. Was he following me?" Martha asked as she looked around.

"Well, in a way. We have a tap on your phone," he whispered. "It will come off as soon as we put the pieces of this puzzle together. Don't tell anyone—not even Winnie."

In a few minutes, two detectives arrived. They immediately took lots of photos and made copious notes. They also took Gwen into a side room for questioning. They spent considerable time examining the backdoor.

"Here's how they got in. See this, Lewis? The lock doesn't close all the way. They simply pushed on the door like this." The detective explained as he demonstrated how quickly the vandals gained entrance into the building.

"Gwen, I'll put a call in for maintenance and have them come here and clean this mess. They'll rope this section off so that the children won't be in any danger. Move your low tables over here and arrange some books and toys on them. If they ask where the swans are, tell them that they are getting repaired and will return next week," Martha directed.

Lewis was listening to Martha and he was impressed with her management style. She took over smoothly as she put her hand on Gwen's shoulder. "I'll also request that maintenance put new locks on both doors."

"Thank you, Martha."

"Oh, Gwen, take inventory of the books that were destroyed. We'll need that for the insurance company and for ordering replacements. I'll see what I can do about the swans—the children loved them so much."

Lewis took Martha aside and whispered, "I must tell you— we're doing a background check on your staff."

"Is that necessary?" Martha asked as she winced.

"Sorry, Green Eyes, yes it is. Someone is angry about something. You are precious and I won't take any chances that whoever is doing these things might turn to bodily harm."

Martha took a seat beside Gwen to console her. "Gwen, this was not your fault. Whoever did this certainly must have some kind of mental problem."

"I remember locking the doors—honest, I do," a shaken Gwen said to one of the detectives.

"I'm sure you did. The lock just didn't function properly. Miss Harrison, I would recommend new locks for both doors," he cautioned as he walked away.

"Gwen, I'll stay here until the maintenance crew arrives," Martha said.

Lewis whispered to Martha, "I need to see you alone." As the two of them sauntered to the other side of the room, Lewis said, "Ronald and Cora have invited us to have dinner with them on Valentine's Day at the Logan Country Club. Would you like to go?"

"I'd love that. Lewis, I was so certain that these problems were over, but now I realize that they're getting uglier. Thank you for coming here so quickly," She stood on her toes and kissed his cheek.

"Thank you, Green Eyes," he said as he smiled. "Got to run right now. I have a commissioners' meeting that I must attend. Your carriage will be arriving at your doorstep on Valentine's evening at seven." As he drove away, the feeling of guilt overwhelmed him when he remembered how he had treated Martha the other day. One way or the other, he vowed that he would never act that ridiculously again. He needed to think of something he could do to make it up to her.

CHAPTER 17

February 14, 1972

T HE WORTHINGTONS HAD arrived at Logan Country Club and were seated in an intimate dining room that accommodated only four tables. Anyone, who would be seated there, had a general understanding that everyone wanted privacy at their own table. Tonight was a special one for Ronald and Cora—it was here, in this same room—when Ron had popped the question to Cora. There were bouquets of red roses and flickering heart-shaped candles on each table. And, to Cora's delight, Ronald had not forgotten to hire a harpist. Ronald took Cora's hand, and said, "My precious one, you look just as beautiful as you did when I sat here nervously fingering a ring box in my pocket."

"Thank you, Ronnie. Here come our guests. Let's hope that their romance lasts as long as ours has," Cora said as she gave a little wave to Martha and Lewis as they entered the room.

Ronald stood up and welcomed the couple. "We're pleased to have you join us on this special occasion. Many years ago, as a brash young man, I brought Cora here to propose and thank goodness she said *yes.*"

"What?" Lewis teased. "Reggie allowed you to beat him to the altar?"

"Well, he's already been there three times. I only walked down the aisle one time. Do you think it's time for me to look for wife number two?"

"You do, and I'll beat you to a pulp," Cora said as she kissed her husband's cheek.

"See, Martha, see how I'm abused?" Ronald said, as he placed a small package in front of his wife.

Martha watched as Cora carefully unwrapped it. "Oh, Ronnie, sweetheart, this is gorgeous," she said as she held up a diamond necklace.

The waiter arrived with flutes of champagne. As he held his glass up, Ronald said, "Cora, I thank God for the years he has given me with you. And, dear Lord, if it isn't too much to ask, may I please have many more?"

"Martha, Lewis has told us about the damage that was done to the North Public Library. Cora and I were both devastated that someone would do something that malicious. So, Worthington Capital Partners will provide the funding necessary to replace everything that was damaged as well as the funding needed to make the building burglar-proof. At the same time, we realize that there are three other branches of the library that are also in need of updating resources. I know that law enforcement will do everything possible to catch these wretches. We just want you to know that you have one million dollars to use for your libraries."

"I don't know how to respond," Martha said breathlessly. "My staff and I appreciate your kindness and..." Martha couldn't talk any more for the tears were getting in her way.

"Martha, I know that you shared some of your thoughts about being a librarian with me, but can you tell us what you like best about your job?" Cora asked.

Martha wiped away her tears. "From the time I was a

little girl, I loved books. While my dad always encouraged me to read, I lost both of my parents when I was nine. I then lived with my Aunt Ivy, where I was terribly unhappy and neglected. I found a haven at the local library and quickly became friendly with the librarian. Also, when I found that I liked order, the Dewey Decimal System provided that. I knew that I had found my calling."

"You certainly impressed Reggie. He said that he's going to check out his local librarian to see if she's as wonderful as you are," Cora teased.

The four diners were having a marvelous time together. Cora was already wearing her new necklace, while Martha was looking forward to sharing the good news with her staff members. Lewis reached into his jacket pocket and pulled out a small jewelry box. He turned to Martha and said, "Green Eyes, this belonged to my grandmother."

Martha opened the little box while her hands shook. There, nestled in the satin lining was an engraved gold locket with a flower motif. "Cora insisted I put my picture in it,"

"Oh, how charming. How thoughtful of you, my darling."

When the harpist played *Stardust,* Ronald and Cora began to dance. Ronald waved his arms at Martha and Lewis, indicating that he wanted them to join in. As the soft gentle notes filled the little room, no one could deny that love was wrapped around every note.

⇔ CHAPTER 18 ⇔

March 4, 1972

"Lewis, there's so much work going on in my libraries now that construction and remodeling are taking place," Martha said as she poured a cup of hot tea for him.

"How's Stanley getting along with the others now that you have given him some additional duties?"

"Very well. He seems to be pleased with his new status. He's a good person, and we have already begun planning what we're going to do to honor the Worthingtons when we have our open house."

The only noise that could be heard for a while was the clanking of their teaspoons hitting the sides of the cups. Lewis broke the silence first. "Martha, tell me about what you experienced when you lived with your aunt. That is, if it won't make you sad."

"It's okay. The first time that I walked into Ivy's home, I saw darkness in contrast to my home that had always been bright and cheery. I had taken a few things with me to console myself as I kept to my bedroom most of the time. I seldom went into the kitchen since it was always cluttered, chaotic and not quite clean. When I got older, I would try to clean the dirty dishes out of the sink and wipe off the table. My bedroom, however, was my sanctuary for my aunt's acerbic tongue and a place to express my imagination and creative energies. In addition to the beautiful vanity set that had belonged to my dad's aunt, I also had a long hat pin, several lace handkerchiefs, a black evening purse, and a box of beautiful sashes that I could use as belts. I guess it's safe to say that I became obsessed with those items—they somehow gave me the comfort that I needed so desperately."

Lewis reached across the table and took Martha's hand. "My Green Eyes, you're so very precious to me. You'll never be lonely again, for no matter where I might have to travel, you can always depend on me to come home to you. Now, I think it's time for me to share some things about me with you. I've learned a lot about what your job entails, now you need to know more about what I do for Ronald."

"I don't know, Lewis, it all seems so complicated," Martha said hesitantly.

"Ronald is a venture capitalist. His company looks for small, early-stage, emerging firms that are deemed to have high-growth potential in expectation that the company will sell that firm once its value peaks. Let's say that you started a company to make widgets—everyone loves widgets and wants some—but for some reason your company is not making a profit. Ronald comes along; he understands that people want widgets, but they seem to overlook the ones you make. He offers you a big price and buys your company. You sell it. Ronald then brings in the people who know how to change your widget and market it to the right people. When Ronald believes that the company has gone as far as it can, he sells it at a profit."

"Is all of this legal?"

"Yes. However, there are those out there who don't always

offer the owners a fair price. But, that's not illegal either. Ronald, however, is always fair."

"I remember that one time you told me that you were Ronald's *hound dog*. So, does that mean that you search for the right opportunities for him to buy?"

"You got it. The old saying, *It takes money to make money* is true."

"Where do Ronald's brother and son fit into all of this?"

"They are both partners in the organization. Reggie is perfectly happy with the arrangement, since he makes money all the time without lifting a finger. He does, however, comes to the board meetings, and, surprisingly, sometimes he even makes a good suggestion. Ronald's son, Matthew, is currently running the branch we have in Zurich. Ronnie has offered me the position of Chairman of the Ronald and Cora Worthington Foundation."

"That sounds important."

"You bet it is. What I like best about this opportunity is that it makes me a partner in the firm. I can call the shots and travel only when I really need to. I need to tell you that I have resigned as a commissioner. Rocco's brother-in-law will be replacing me. Ronald brought it to my attention that, if I stayed on as a commissioner, I might be challenged about my relationship with you."

"Why?"

"Because you report to the commissioners, my love. Besides, it was only a temporary appointment. Now, I have something to tell you."

"Oh, that doesn't sound good," Martha said hesitantly.

"I have to go away for a couple of weeks. It's time that we get Matthew out of Zurich and get him ready to take over for Ronald. We need to take care of some sticky business before we can do that. Matthew will need help, but the good part of all this is that I will then take over the Foundation which means much less traveling for me. I estimate that sometime in late March—early April, I'll be back."

Martha was quiet at first. "Lewis, I will miss you, but I realize that you have important things to take care of."

"You're my most important thing," Lewis said as he knelt beside her.

"Thank you, Lewis. I would wait a thousand years for you, Lewis. I love you."

On the other side of town, Mookey and Fat Tony were sitting in a run-down diner having breakfast. "Mookey, how come Mack doesn't give us anything to do? I'm getting bored just sitting around."

"Mack will be out of commission for a few weeks. He had some kind of operation and needs to recuperate. He's still sending us money, so don't complain."

"How long?"

"How long what?" Mookey snarled.

"How long must we wait to do something?"

"Damn it, Fat Tony, I don't know. Pick up a babe—or something—but stop bugging me."

CHAPTER 19

April 3, 1972

M ARTHA WAS JUST about ready to leave her home to go to work when her doorbell rang. She couldn't imagine who it could be. As she opened the door, and saw a smiling Lewis standing on her stoop, she was shocked. "Lewis!" she yelled as he picked her up and swung her in a circle.

"Wow, Green Eyes, you didn't forget me," he said as he gave her a long, passionate kiss. "Martha, my Martha—how I missed you."

As the two of them struggled to get into the house, while they were laughing, staying glued together, Lewis was finally able to slam the door closed with his foot. "You are so stunning, my Book Lady. I never want to be away from you that long again!"

"I have all your postcards taped to my closet door," Martha laughed. "You know, just like a teenager."

"Oh, you are definitely *not* a teenager. You are perfect in every way."

"I wish I didn't have to go to work, but some inspectors are going to be at the West Branch to check on updates."

"I'll be back to pick you up at six and we'll go somewhere romantic for dinner. And then, if I play my cards right, you'll invite me to come home with you," Lewis said as he hugged her again. "I have a surprise to give you."

"A surprise—what is it?"

"No, a surprise is a surprise. Now, I'll let you go to work with the inspectors. Give 'em' hell, Martha."

Martha thought that six o'clock would never come. Finally, she heard his car pull up and she opened the front door.

"Ah, madam, it seems that I have found the right place," Lewis said. "I was told the most beautiful woman in the world lives here."

Martha smiled and replied, "Oh, sorry, sir, but she lives down the block."

Lewis took her in his arms and said, "Well, then, I guess I'll just have to take you out for dinner."

After they were seated in the restaurant, Lewis ordered drinks and said, "Martha, we are going on a trip."

Martha looked confused. "But you just came home from a trip."

"Oh, I know that, but now is the time for me to do something really special for you. But I'm not telling you where we're going just yet."

"But how will I be able to pack if I don't know where we'll be going?"

"Let's see," Lewis said as he paused. "I think you'll need your passport, walking shoes, and a sweater. Oh, you'll also need raingear. We'll be taking the Worthington plane."

"I didn't know Worthington owned a plane," Martha said as she registered surprise. "Wow that must have cost a huge fortune."

"It's so much easier than trying to get all his people to places using commercial flights. Financial deals don't always hang around too long and we must get there when the timing is right. And, along with the work we do for Ronald, we generally haul medical supplies and such in the hold for humanitarian needs around the world. While Ronald is an astute and tough businessman, he also has a warm and caring nature. He lucked out in getting the plane though. He had the opportunity to buy a Boeing 707—when a wealthy Japanese businessman ran into very bad financial times. I personally believe he did the guy a favor."

"My head is spinning. Lewis you constantly amaze me."

"Oh, I hope so. I hear that amazement often turns into lifelong love."

The next morning, as soon as Martha entered her office, she flew into action. First, she called Stanley Barber and asked him to meet her for lunch. She needed to speak with him about taking over for her while she was gone. Opening her briefcase, she lined up the things she needed to complete this week. The morning flew by, but she was pleased at the progress she had made in filling out the endless forms that she then forwarded to the commissioners.

As she walked into the restaurant, she spotted Stanley, looking very nice in a dark blue blazer, white shirt, and a striped tie, seated at a table. "Hello, Stanley, thank you for meeting me on such short notice," Martha said as she placed a file folder on her lap.

"Anytime, Martha. This happens to be my favorite restaurant. However, I am curious as to why I'm here," he said as he fussed with his tie.

"I'll be taking a long week-end trip and I'm putting you in charge while I'm gone. All of my calls on Friday and Monday will be forwarded to you. After we have finished our lunch, I would appreciate your looking over the forms I have brought with me. You can take the folder along and look through it at your leisure. If you have any questions, please feel free to call me."

"Thank you, Martha. I'm more than happy to help out."

Stanley tried hard not to show too much enthusiasm—after all, he would be in charge for only two days. He never told Martha how extremely disappointed he had been when the commissioners chose her instead of him to be the Director of Public Libraries in Logan County. After all, Martha didn't have a family to support like he did. Or, they might have chosen her simply because she was considered handicapped. Stanley thought it was ridiculous to call Martha's little limp a handicap—she gets around just fine. But, who knew what might happen—his opportunity might come before too long—after all, he had heard that she was dating the wealthy Lewis Holmes, who was part of the Worthington dynasty.

❧ CHAPTER 20 ❧

April 13, 1972

I T WAS ALMOST eight thirty when Lewis and Martha drove through the corporate gate at the airport. They were scheduled to take off at nine. After entering a small building, they were required to show their passports at the check-in counter but, unlike the procedure used when flying regular commercial, they merely dropped their bags, which were quickly whisked away. Martha followed Lewis as he led the way to the tarmac where Captain Anthony Tobias greeted them warmly. "Good evening, Mr. Holmes—Miss Harrison. We're promised perfect flying weather tonight."

"Nice to see you again, Toby. By the way, I hear that congratulations are in order since there is now a Mrs. Tobias," Lewis said as he shook the captain's hand.

"Thanks, Mr. Holmes. I chased her until she finally caught me," he said as he smiled and began his inspection of the aircraft.

Martha was amazed at how large the plane was. There certainly had to be other passengers, but she hadn't noticed any. As she stepped into the plane, she saw several rows of leather seats, an oval conference table and more leather chairs, a lounging area with sofas and chairs, a bar, a lavatory, and a galley. It certainly was different from any other plane she had ever been on.

The attendant greeted them and then said, "Welcome aboard, Mr. Holmes –Miss Harrison. As soon as the aircraft is at cruising speed, I'll serve dinner. Meanwhile, may I offer you a drink?"

"How about champagne, Elaine. We're in a celebratory mood," Lewis replied.

Martha whispered to Lewis, "Are we the only passengers?"

Lewis leaned over and kissed her cheek. "Well, except for the captain, his co-pilot, the navigator, and the attendant, yes."

"Will you tell me now where we're going?"

"I'll give you a hint—we'll be heading north," Lewis replied.

"Lewis, it's too early to visit Santa," Martha said as she laughed.

Martha was overcome with happiness. She had lived so long believing that her job was the only reward in life that she was entitled to. Hoping with all her heart that she was the only woman, who had taken such a trip with Lewis, she childishly crossed her fingers. She remembered the advice that Cora had given her—*run with it*. I must stop my negative thinking and put myself into Lewis's hands.

The lovers slowly sipped their drinks, taking time out for kissing. Elaine interrupted them with dinner that was served in the lounge area with white linens, crystal, and flowers.

Over dinner, Lewis said, "I won't keep you in the dark any longer, Martha. We're going to Haworth, England, which I am sure you know is referred to as Bronte Country. You'll have an opportunity to visit the places you only read about. While, personally, I wish Emily Bronte had written a different ending for *Wuthering Heights*, I'm here to show you just how much I love you."

Martha sat stoic for a moment. "Did you say Haworth, England?" she asked as she grabbed the arms of her seat. "Lewis, you're a darling. I never dreamed that we would be going there. You're unbelievable."

Lewis slid off his chair and knelt in front of her. "No, don't cry, my love. I know that Bronte is your favorite author. You have talked about how Catherine and Heathcliff fell in love as they scampered over the moors, so I felt that you deserved to see where all of that happened."

Martha wrapped her arms around Lewis. "I'm so grateful, Lewis. You couldn't have chosen a more emotional spot in the entire world for this trip. Thank you...thank you."

The lovebirds were interrupted when Captain Tobias appeared to wish them a goodnight. "Elaine will get your couches ready. She'll serve you a light breakfast in the morning. We'll arrive at the airport at nine local time."

When Martha finally got under the covers on her couch, she lifted herself up on her elbows. "Lewis, I don't know what to say. You are so thoughtful and loving that I can hardly catch my breath."

"Sweetheart," he said as he kissed her. "You may be wondering if I have ever taken anyone else on a trip like this—the answer is *no*. Martha, you mean everything to me. I think it's time to tell you about my past. I have never been married, engaged, or in a serious relationship. Yes, I dated. But, I was never able to find someone who loved me for me and not the fact that I am related to the Worthingtons."

"Lewis, what did you say?" a surprised Martha asked. "How?"

"I thought that Cora would have told you that. My mother and Cora are sisters. When I lost both of my parents, I went to live with my Aunt Cora at the mansion. Lewis paused and studied her face for a moment and said, "Martha, it's hard to imagine that two people, each of whom lost their parents when they were children, meet and fall in love. From the first time that you smiled at me, not knowing who I was, I was smitten. And, when I covered your body at the Holiday Hop, I just knew that I had finally found my soul mate. So, in a way, I am a bit like Heathcliff. But, unlike that dumb guy, I'm not going anywhere. Martha Harrison, I love you."

"I love you, too, Lewis. While I've been hesitant to say those words, and I still have deep-seated fears that someone will take this away from me, I turn myself over to you. I finally agree with you—Heathcliff should have stayed with his ladylove.

"Now, my darling, we better get some sleep. We have a busy day ahead of us," Lewis said, as he pulled up Martha's cover and kissed her forehead.

Lewis finally lay down on his couch. As he stared at the ceiling of the plane, he thought about the little box he had in his valise. Recently, when Ronald was preparing him for a business trip to New York City, Lewis had confided in him that he was going to ask Martha to marry him but had no idea where to get a ring that she would like. Ronald immediately picked up the phone and called Harry Winston, the top dealer of vintage jewelry in New York City, and got Lewis an appointment to see him. It was not like any other jewelry store that Lewis had visited. Lewis was escorted into a small intimate area with two chairs and a glass-top table and no displays of rows and rows of jewels. Harry brought out a small salver with just three rings displayed on the velvet tray. Lewis immediately spotted the one he wanted: a slim platinum band with filigree on the sides. Nestled in the center was an exquisite round-cut, Columbian emerald. Almost as gorgeous as Martha's eyes. The side stones were brilliant cut diamonds. He chuckled when he remembered what Ronald had told him, *"Lewis, your woman loves vintage. If you want a happy marriage, you better remember that."*

Perhaps he should wake her now and propose. Then, he thought better of that idea. She loved the moors. That's where he might be brave enough to ask her.

High up in the air, two lovers were lost in sleep as the plane moved through the star-laden night sky.

CHAPTER 21

April 14, 1972

MARTHA HEARD A soft chime and assumed it was the attendant letting them know that it was time to rise and shine. She gently leaned over and touched Lewis' arm. "I believe we need to join the rest of the world, my love."

After he managed to sit upright, Lewis said, "I better fill you in on where we're going next. We'll be staying at a private home that's about 25 miles from the airport. The property is owned by Nigel Hall, a client of the Worthington Group, who is currently in South Africa. Martha, you're going to love it. It's a Georgian stone house and the property is a working farm that produces wheat and barley. The home is rich in history. It was once owned by the Towneley family of Burnley, who retained extensive estates in and around Lancashire and Yorkshire. The property is managed by a typical English couple, Mr. and Mrs. Dewhirst. I'm fairly certain that Mr. Dewhirst will be waiting for us."

As Martha was combing her hair, she turned around and said, "I'm still afraid that this is all a dream—one from which I don't want to wake up."

"Good morning, folks. I brought you coffee and rolls. If

there is anything else that I can do for you, just ring the bell," Elaine said as she retreated to the galley.

"Not too much on this tray," Lewis said as he looked over what the attendant had brought, "but, I promise you a wonderful English breakfast a little later."

While they were going through immigration, their luggage was loaded into a car on the tarmac. Martha felt like a little child on Christmas morning. She was so excited that she could hardly contain herself. Finally, she was introduced to Mr. Dewhirst and liked him instantly. Her heart almost stopped when he pulled the car onto the highway and got in the left lane before she realized that that was how traffic moved in England.

Martha was charmed by the green pastures, hosting sheep and an abundance of lambs. The country road they were traveling wandered between limestone walls and barley fields, and little bridges that spanned streams, and rills, and becks. She was thrilled when she spotted the beautiful dales and hills that were either nearly flat or gently rounded.

"Martha, what you're looking at are the Pennines, a chain of hills that form a more-or-less continuous range. The Pennines lay north to south and are often called the backbone of England," Lewis explained.

When they arrived at the home, Mrs. Dewhirst greeted Lewis warmly. "Oh, Mr. Holmes, I'm so happy to see you again. How long has it been?"

"I was here last year for grouse hunting. This beautiful woman is Martha Harrison." While Mrs. Dewhirst made a fuss over Martha, she ushered her to a pretty bedroom. She then guided Lewis to an adjoining room. Lewis smiled and winked at Martha, as he thanked his hostess.

"After you freshen up, Luv, please come down for an

English breakfast, There's nowt like a proper brew." Mrs. Dewhirst said as she scurried away.

When they went downstairs, they were delighted to see that they would be having breakfast by the fireplace. While it was going to be a sunny day, there was a sight chill in the air, so the warmth from the fireplace was appreciated. Martha was surprised to see so much food. There was cereal and fresh fruit, bacon, eggs, grilled tomatoes, mushrooms, toast, marmalade and tea.

After they finished breakfast, they toured the farm. "This part of England is widely considered to be one of the most scenic areas of Britain," Lewis said. "I read that in a travel brochure," he confessed.

To her right, Martha saw a patch of deciduous woodland— so green—at this time of the year. To her left, she saw a checkerboard of wheat and barley fields, juxtaposed with fallow pastures that were awash in the colors of wildflowers: pinks, and yellows, and blues. It was everything she thought it would be—and more.

A farmhand approached to alert them that an activity was about to unfold that Martha might like to witness. He said that a flock of sheep would be coming down to the barn for ear-tagging, and then pointed to a small figure of a man and his two Border Collies on one of the hilly pastures. They watched as the man gestured to the dogs. When the flock got closer, Martha could hear that he was giving them commands. What Martha saw next looked like a ballet. The man used a hand signal and the collies responded by interacting with the sheep. The dogs stayed behind the flock and Martha could tell that she was watching a special working partnership between man and dog. The dogs were calm and controlling, keeping the sheep moving into a tight, cohesive herd by crouching and staring and, occasionally, barking. Eventually, the shepherd seemed satisfied as the whole herd moved toward the barn. A cacophony of bleating from the lambs and their mothers, who were temporarily separated as the herd moved, filled the air.

"Lewis, why do the ewes have blotches of paint on their backs? Martha asked.

"The coloring is used for identification—for breeding purposes and for ownership," he explained. "I'd like to show you one more thing today—that is, if you're up to it. However, it will entail a short push iron ride."

Martha readily agreed and soon they were pedaling bicycles down the lane. She noticed that the fields gave way to rising hills that she later learned were called *fells*. When they reached the top of one fell, Lewis pulled over, stretched out his arms and said, "There they are, Martha—Emily Bronte's beloved moors."

At first, Martha held her breath. She couldn't believe that she was actually standing on the moors—the very place where Emily allowed Catherine and Heathcliff to fall in love. Martha turned 360 degrees, not wanting to miss a view, she took several deep breaths as if she could capture the sensation of what she was feeling.

Lewis watched her intently. By her reactions, he knew that she was thrilled at the sight. "Let's park the bikes and walk down this little footpath," Lewis suggested. "This is the oldest hiking path in England. It's 250 miles long."

"After we just flew 3,492 miles to get here, I hope you're not planning on hiking to the end," Martha said as she laughed.

They joined hands and began walking. Martha saw that the moors were covered with a blanket of heather. "Lewis, what a spectacular sight. This must be breathtaking when the heather blooms in August and September. Thank you for bringing me here."

Above their heads, a little bird, seeking attention, twisted and dived, while he sang a little song. "It's not a skylark," Lewis said, "but it sounds great."

Impulsively, Martha said, "Hail to thee, blithe Spirit!"

"I know that line from Shelly's poem," Lewis said proudly.

"You've made a dream come true. I have always wanted to see the sites that thrilled me so when I first read *Wuthering Heights*." She stood in front of him, lifted her head slightly, and they kissed.

Inspired, Lewis got down on one knee and looked up at Martha. As he pulled out the distinctive navy blue leather ring box from his jacket pocket, he held it up so she could see it. "My beloved, while this is what Heathcliff should have done, he didn't. I love you with all my heart and I want to spend the rest of my life telling you that. Martha Harrison, will you marry me?"

Martha was shocked. Here was the man she loved so ardently, asking her to marry him. In the back of her head, she heard Cora's voice, *"Lewis loves you—run with it."*

"Yes...yes...yes..." she whispered.

"Was that a *yes*?" Lewis teased.

"It was three of them," Martha said joyously.

Lewis stood up. He took the ring out of the box, and, as his hand shook, he slipped it on her finger. They embraced.

As the wind grew stronger, Lewis said, "I wish we could stay in this spot longer, but the clouds are moving in rapidly. We need to head back as quickly as possible." Hand-in-hand, they ran and retrieved their bikes and began pedaling as fast as they could. But, the heavens opened, and the rain came down sideways. The lovers almost seemed oblivious to the downpour as they jumped off their bikes and hurried to the doorway where Mrs. Dewhirst was anxiously waiting for their return.

As they entered the house, Mrs. Dewhirst tossed large towels over their shoulders. "I put terry robes on your beds for you to wear to come down for high tea. Just put your wet things in the bathroom and I'll get them later."

Shortly, Martha and Lewis were downstairs warm and snug in their robes. "Martha, would it be alright with you if I told Mrs. Dewhirst the good news?"

"Certainly. She'll be the first to know," Martha said softly.

"I'll make sure that Reggie knows, so he understands that you are taken," Lewis teased.

"Oh, Lewis. I suppose I could have run away with him, but I didn't," Martha said lightheartedly. "Lewis, what is high tea?" she whispered.

"High tea is meant for the working man who comes home after working all day and is as hungry as a bear. Afternoon teas are social things and much less food is served."

Mrs. Dewhirst announced the meal. Martha was impressed with what she saw. There was Shepherd's Pie, Yorkshire ham slices, along with peas and carrots, and a wonderful side dish called Rock Cakes that reminded Martha of pancakes, Wensleydale cheese and crackers, which Lewis said was usually included. For dessert, they could choose from spiced rhubarb crumble or ginger cake.

Mrs. Dewhirst came in to say goodnight. "Thank you so much, Mrs. Dewhirst for the wonderful high tea," Lewis said. "We want to share some good news with you. Miss Harrison has accepted my proposal of marriage, and you're the first one to know."

Mrs. Dewhirst beamed and said. "Oh, I'm reight chuffed for ye."

Lewis whispered to Martha, "She said she's so happy for us."

"Thank you," Martha said happily. "Would you like to see my ring?" Martha asked as she held her hand out.

"Beautiful, simply gorgeous," Mrs. Dewhirst said as she wiped away a few tears.

After Mrs. Dewhirst left, Martha and Lewis stayed by the fireplace for a while, reminiscing about the remarkable day that they had just experienced. All was perfect with their world.

However, thousands of miles away, chaos was raising its ugly head again as Fat Tony and Mookey entered Martha's home in the dark of night. "I don't know why I had to come along with you to do this job," Fat Tony complained.

"You know what the boss man said. We work everything together, so he knows for sure that we do what he wants done, you dumb ass. Now, go out in the kitchen and turn the water on, while I go upstairs to the bathroom. You think you can do that?" Mookey said disgustingly.

As Mookey leaned into the tub and placed the stopper in position, he wondered how long it would take for the water to start running over the top of the tub and down the stairs. Just like Niagara Falls. When he ran down the steps, he found Fat Tony standing in the living room with a can of spray paint in his hands.

"Look, Mookey, I wrote on the wall," Fat Tony said proudly.

"What the hell is that supposed to be?" Mookey asked.

"You know what that means. I'm calling her a *hore*."

"Dumb ass, you forgot the W!"

"Where?"

"In the front of the word. The correct spelling is W-H-O-R-E."

"That ain't right—but if you say so..." Fat Tony said as he quickly sprayed a W on the wall. "Now, do I get a gold star for spelling?"

⪻ CHAPTER 22 ⪼

April 15, 1972

L EWIS OPENED HIS eyes slowly. He could feel Martha's warm body next to him. He was living in paradise. As he lay there, he wanted to shout out to the world that there was such a thing as *true love*. He thought about the years that had gone by, and how they always seemed empty or lacking something. Now he rationalized that he probably had to go through those barren years in order to understand what he was now experiencing.

She stirred. "Lewis, are you awake?" she said softly.

"Yes, my love. I hope you slept as well as I did."

"So, yesterday wasn't a dream?"

"No, darling—no dream. I believe that since you said *yes* to me that you are stuck with me. I've been told that agreeing to a proposal is absolutely, unequivocally binding. In fact, I also heard that anyone who tries to get out of such an agreement is immediately put in chains and placed in a horrible black tunnel."

Martha sat up. "Lewis, for heaven's sake—where do you get these crazy ideas?"

Lewis gathered her in his arms. "Martha, do you realize that you'll soon be Mrs. Lewis Holmes?"

"But we've only been engaged for one day, Lewis. What do you mean soon?"

"That's all up to you. You tell me when you're ready."

"But, there are so many things that we must discuss. For instance, where are we going to live? What about my job? What kind of wedding do we want? And, children..."

"Oh, children—that one's easy. At least a dozen," Lewis teased as he played with her hair. "But, we need to make sure that we know how to do that."

"Lewis!"

"Baby, I love you up to the moon," Lewis said. "I've never been this happy—I owe that all to you. How about this—we'll pick one subject each day until we get all of our issues settled."

"Good idea. I'll let you pick the topic for today," Martha said as she kissed his forehead.

"Okay. Where are we going to live—topic for today? I live on the Worthington compound in a home that Cora and Ronald gave to my mother after my dad died. When we get home, I'll take you to see it. If you don't like it, or you would rather not live there, we'll make other plans."

"You never stop surprising me. Okay, I agree with that. Now, come here and let me whisper sweet nothings in your ear," Martha said as she pulled the covers off.

An hour or so later, the two of them finally made their way downstairs for breakfast. Martha was delighted that Mrs. Dewhirst had prepared a simple tray of fruit, ginger cake, and tea. "This is perfect," Lewis said. "We can stop along the way today at some little shop in Haworth."

Mr. Dewhirst was waiting in the car for them. As they rode along, Martha discovered that the area was extremely hilly. When they arrived in Haworth and she saw how steep Main Street was, Martha was glad that Mr. Dewhirst was going to pick them up at the bottom of the hill. When she got out of the car, she saw the distant moors, the lush green valleys, and the quaint shops and homes, decorated with flowers in window boxes and pots of flowers at doorways—everything was the way she had envisioned.

"This is the Bronte Parsonage and Museum," Lewis said as they came to a Greystone Georgian that sat high above Haworth. "It's between Haworth and the wild moors beyond," Lewis added. "The parsonage, the church, and graveyard all sit on the very top of the hill. I think that's a bit odd."

Martha now understood why the Bronte family had been so influenced by the moors. She knew that the family had consisted of three girls: Emily, Charlotte, and Anne, and one boy, Branwell. When Martha realized that Emily had died at age 30, it jolted her senses. She thought, *'I'm 30!'* She wondered, if Emily had lived longer, would she have written more novels and would they all have been sad.

The house looked as if it were waiting for the sisters to return any minute. The rooms were decorated with 19th century furniture, including the writing desks belonging to each of them. Tiny manuscript books, that were on display, allowed visitors to see their handwriting. The dining room was furnished with pieces bought by Charlotte from the royalties she had received from her book *Jane Eyre*.

Other rooms were filled with Bronte personal items, including Charlotte's wedding bonnet, samplers and drawings by Emily as well as drawings of pets. Martha looked out the window and saw a house on the distant moor. The tour guide told her it was called *Top Withens* and that many believe it was the model for Heathcliff's home. She called Lewis over to share this piece of information.

"I hope that's not where you want to live," he whispered in her ear.

She laughed and took his arm as they walked out of the museum. They followed the same footpath that the Brontes had used that led to the church and the graveyard which was enclosed with a black iron fence. The tombstones were weathered and green with moss. Martha was reminded of Thomas Gray's *Elegy Written in a Country Churchyard.*

As they entered St. Michael's and All Angels' Church, Martha said, "I'm surprised at how small this church is since it was a parish church. Look, Lewis, there is a Bronte Chapel with a crocheted kneeler and candles to light."

The tour guide explained that the chandelier and the altar were from the original church. He pointed out a bronze plaque, stating that all the family members except Anne were buried in the crypt below. He also called attention to a beautiful stained-glass window that had been commissioned by an American admirer in honor of Charlotte.

"Would you like to take a break, Martha? We could sit here on a bench, or better yet, what do you say about going to the *Black Bull Inn,* where Emily's brother used to imbibe?"

The pub was quite crowded, but they managed to get two seats. Lewis went to the bar and ordered a pint for himself and tea for Martha. It was an interesting stop because Martha felt almost like a regular as they rested and discussed the things that they had seen, while they enjoyed a lunch of fish and chips.

After lunch, they waked down the pavement and visited various shops, including a chocolate shop, where they bought salted toffee and coconut truffles. At a quaint tea shop, Martha bought a tin of tea and a tea strainer. "This will be a special gift for Winnie."

When Lewis saw an upscale china shop, he insisted they go in. "Martha, would you like an English bone china tea set? Just pick the pattern you like. It will be the first thing we buy together for our home."

"Lewis, you're so sweet. Thank you, darling. Now, I can invite Cora and Ronald for tea some time," Martha said as she kissed him. Turning to the shop girl she said, "I would like to purchase six of those adorable china bells, please."

"Souvenirs?" Lewis asked.

The last stop for the day was the train station in Haworth for the *Keighley and Worth Valley Railroad*, a restored railroad line that ran from Keighley to Oxenhope through Haworth. When Lewis and Martha arrived, tourists were taking photos of the red painted building with yellow trim. Flowers in pots at the front door added to its charm of the little village station. To Martha's delight, the station even had the famous red British phone box outside of the building.

"You know, Lewis, I've seen pictures of this train station, but it really comes to life seeing it in person," Martha said. "In fact, I think I have one in my collection."

When Mr. Dewhirst picked them up and took them back to Nigel Hall's country home, Martha said, "Lewis that was so much fun. Thank you."

Lewis said, to Mr. Dewhirst, "We're as happy as a pig in muck."

Mr. Dewhirst broke out in laughter. 'Oh, aye!"

Lewis whispered to Martha, "I told him that we were as happy as pigs in muck."

"Lewis, would it be alright to ask Mrs. Dewhirst to just bring us a tray tonight rather than a dinner? I'm ready to relax and sit back to talk about our wonderful day."

"Sweetheart, yes. Later, if you feel like a moonlight walk,

we can do that. Perhaps we could stroll down to the canal and watch the water fowl and enjoy the sound of the little waterfall. Anything you want."

Meanwhile, back in the States, Martha's neighbor was listening to the sound of a waterfall of a different sort. She was prompted to call her son. "Barry, can you run over here and check something out for me?...I hear water running next door and I know that Martha is in England."

⇜ CHAPTER 23 ⇝

April 16, 1972

"Mrs. Dewhirst, we plan to have lunch at a local restaurant, but we will be back for dinner," Lewis said as he and Martha were having breakfast. "We appreciate your kindness as well as your culinary skills. You are making this trip one that we'll never forget."

"Thank you, Mr. Holmes. I do hope you'll be back some day. Maybe to celebrate an anniversary," she smiled and looked at the two of them over the top of her spectacles. "Do you have a tour guide for today?"

"For the morning, yes. But, I thought we would enjoy just being on our own this afternoon," Lewis explained. "I think Mr. Dewhirst is waiting for us," he said as he reached for Martha's hand.

As Lewis helped her into the car, Martha said, "Good morning, Mr. Dewhirst. What's your weather report for the day?"

"I predict sunshine and a slight breeze," he said as they drove away. "At least that's what they said on the telly this morning."

They picked up their tour guide, Jane Harkin, and headed to Bronte Waterfalls. As they got out of the car, Jane said,

"While these falls are small compared to some you have back in the States, you have to agree that they are of outstanding beauty."

After spending considerable time just gazing at Mother Nature at her finest, they headed off to Bronte Bridge. When Martha got a glimpse of the charming stone bridge that local legend said was where the Bronte sisters discussed their stories, she felt closer to the women than ever before. Even if the local lore was not true, Martha was going to believe it anyway.

Just a little further on Pennine Way, Martha was delighted to finally get a close-up view of *Top Withens,* the property that was the model used for Heathcliff's home. However, there really wasn't too much to see since the farmhouse was destroyed in a terrific storm in the late 1880s.

Lewis looked over the ruins. "What a shame. Heathcliff just had a lot of bad luck, didn't he?" he teased.

"Lewis, why are you so hard on him?"

"Sweetie, making a mistake is one thing, but dumb is forever."

Martha broke out in laughter. "Oh, Lewis, I love you."

The tour guide then directed them to Yorkshire Dales National Park where Martha, once again, could view open moorland. She was surprised when they spied red grouse. "Look, Lewis, look!" she said excitedly.

When they arrived at Skipton Castle, Martha was in awe. The 900-year-old Norman castle, with its six massive round towers, had survived since the 14th century. "It's one of the most complete and best preserved medieval castles in England," Jane stated. "See the marks on those stones? The stonemasons would put their marks on each stone that they had completed because that's how they were paid. During the

English Civil War, it was one of the main Royalist garrisons in the north. After the castle surrendered to the Roundheads in 1645, Oliver Cromwell ordered for its roof to be removed and it remained open to the elements for more than a decade until Lady Anne Clifford, who was born at the castle, was given permission to restore it on the condition that the castle would no longer bear canons."

The three of them explored the castle and viewed the large banquet hall. They descended into the depths of its dungeons. "I wish I could climb to the top of the watch tower like those people are doing. The sight must be breathtaking from up there," Martha said as she hung on to Lewis' arm.

"Martha, would you like to take a boat trip on the canal? I've been told that there are a number of buildings that were part of the textile industry during the 19th century. You must be tired after all that walking," a concerned Lewis said.

"Oh, yes, let's do that."

"Miss Harkin, thank you for being our guide, but we'll take it from here." Lewis said.

After they climbed into the boat, Martha and Lewis cuddled. "Oh, this feels wonderful," Martha said as she planted a kiss on Lewis' cheek."

They learned that the canal covers 127 miles and had been used to transport coal and stone originally, but later, became important in the movement of goods from the mills. Martha was thrilled when she saw a number of swans in the canal.

As they floated along the canal, they began talking about some of the sights they saw. "Lewis, as we sit here, in the middle of all this history, don't you wonder what the people were really like? You know, their ordinary lives. Did they have the same problems and concerns just with different names?"

"Tough question. I think from the time man was put on

this earth, his main concern was food, clothing, and shelter. I'm not too sure that many people who first built this canal, had time for love and romance. Oh, the sex thing was there, but actually, love, true love, might not have existed."

"Maybe that's true. I know I lived a life before I met you, but I can barely remember that now. You made me whole, Lewis. You made me understand what life is really about. Thank you, darling."

"Martha, I could do this all day—sitting here with you, surrounded by historical buildings, and knowing that many others before us did the same thing, is exciting. I love you, Green Eyes."

When they finally stepped out of the boat, they walked down the pavement, hand-in-hand. "It's time for lunch, so you choose where we eat. Sunday meals are always special in this part of the country."

"How about that one—the one with all the flowers outside," Martha said.

Martha was pleased that the restaurant was as adorable as the outside was. In just a few minutes, they were sitting at a table by a window that allowed them to *people-watch* as they ate. After a lunch of roast beef and Yorkshire pudding with horseradish, carrots and peas, they were delighted when the dessert was apple pie with a slice of Wensleydale cheese.

As they strolled through the town, they came to a small park where they found a gazebo. Sitting side by side, they began to share their thoughts about the sights that they had seen that day. "Martha, of all the places we visited, do you have a favorite?"

"I would have to say, I have three favorites—one, of course, are the moors—I will never forget them. I no longer have to wonder what they are like. The second one is the footpath to the Bronte crypt. While I was on that path, my emotions took over and I felt a closeness to the Brontes that will always remain with me. Of course, the most outstanding sight was Skipton Castle. While I often imagined what a real castle would look like, I was not ready for something so formidable. To think of the number of years that that castle stood there, and the people that were swirling around it, is almost impossible However, the best sight of all—no matter where we went—is you, my love."

Lewis sat perfectly still. He took Martha's hands in his and kissed them. While he had been unable to completely appreciate the sights they had seen, the fact that they had made her so happy was all he needed. "I don't know what I did to deserve you, but whatever it was, I'm glad that I found you. We'll go back to the house and rest a bit. And, then in the evening, we'll visit Bingley Arms, a well-known public house where we'll have fish and chips and British ale. It's in the town of Bardsley and dates back to 953 and is mentioned in the *Doomsday Book* of 1086. You got to admit, that's old. We can drink a toast to our trip and perhaps begin to plan a wedding."

Martha had no idea that at this moment her house was filled with workers, who were tirelessly trying to restore the rugs and hardwood floors to their original beauty.

⇜ CHAPTER 24 ⇝

April 17, 1972

Mrs. Dewhirst was delighted that Lewis and Martha enjoyed their breakfast even though it was a bit early. "My Mister is planning on taking you for another look at the moors before he heads to the airport. I enjoyed having you here, Luv."

Martha gave Mrs. Dewhirst a warm hug and kissed her check. "Thank you for everything. We loved staying here and all the attention you gave us."

"Well, it's not every day that couples get engaged when they come here. I wish you a long and happy marriage," Mrs. Dewhirst said as she wiped a tear from her cheek.

Mr. Dewhirst opened the car door for Martha. "Just a minute, Mr. Holmes, I'll open the boot for your bags. I thought it might be mizzlin' today but it's not. So, no misty fog will ruin your last look at the moors."

As they neared a spot where the moors were visible, Martha said, "There they are, Lewis. Oh, look, there's a doe with a fawn by her side. You know that means good luck— we'll be back some day," she said as she took Lewis' hand.

Lewis smiled. "Anything you want, my love. Anything."

When they pulled into the airport, Worthington's plane

was easy to spot. As Mr. Dewhirst helped them out of the car, he shook Lewis' hand and said, "Mind."

Lewis smiled and replied, "We'll try to be careful. Tarra."

"What?" Martha asked as she waved to Mr. Dewhirst.

"He said we should be careful. And instead of saying goodbye they say *tarra*."

Captain Tobias greeted them and said, "Once again, we'll have smooth flying weather. You'll be pleased to know that we were able to deliver the food and medical supplies that we had in the hold without any problems—can't tell you where, though."

"That's great, Toby. I suppose that such deliveries don't always go that way," Lewis said.

"There have been times when we were not allowed to land. But, we have to keep on trying to help. So, now, let's get you home. We take off at 11 and shortly after that, you'll be served lunch. Flying time will be 7 hours 50 minutes. Local time when we land will be 1:50 p.m. If you would like a drink, please let Elaine know."

"By the way, Toby. I have news. Miss Harrison has accepted my proposal. We went to see the moors, so I told her that unless she agreed to marry me, I would abandon her there," Lewis said as he chuckled.

"Lewis, you tell such terrible tales," Martha said as she laughed.

"Congratulations, you two. Mr. Holmes, you're a lucky man," Toby said as he headed for the cockpit.

As they sat down, Lewis said, "You know, my love, we have lots to talk about on the way home. Remember, we already dealt with one issue and that was children. I think we decided on a dozen."

"Lewis, we will have children, but I'm not sure if it will be 12. Let's just take it one at a time," Martha said as she smiled.

"Okay. Now, let's talk about your job. When you think about your job, what are your plans? Did you ever dream about trying something new?"

"Well, you know that I love being a librarian. However, in my dreams, I have often thought about opening a vintage business. Something like Nickles but with high-end items and designing services."

"Designing?" Lewis asked.

"If someone wanted, let's say, a living room, or a bedroom, or a side room, to be a celebration of vintage furnishings and accessories, I would do that," Martha explained. "Why do you ask?"

"You're going to have to get used to having money. If you keep your current job, people might not like the fact that you now have money and you're working in a job that someone else might want or really need."

"You have money, Lewis—not me."

"You have money right now. We own everything together. If you would prefer not to work at all, that's fine with me. But, if you would like to try your vintage dream, you could do that."

"Lewis, I'm not marrying you for your money. I'm marrying you for you," Martha argued.

"Ronald was my advisor and as soon as I bought the ring, I made you my partner," Lewis responded.

"But, what if I change my mind and I don't marry you?"

"We are soul mates—I know that—you know that," Lewis said as he took her in his arms and kissed her. They were quiet for several minutes. "You don't have to leave your job right away, but you could give a six-month notice. That would be more than fair. I bet you that Stanley will be jumping up and down to hear about that. Close your eyes, babe, just think about it for a while."

Elaine served them drinks and then said, "Captain Tobias said that congratulations are in order." When Martha showed her the ring, Elaine oohed and aahed at all the right places. When Elaine walked away, she thought to herself that Martha had what every girl dreamed of—she had hit the jackpot. After all, Lewis Holmes was extremely attractive, intelligent, and well-connected. Most importantly, just by watching him, anyone could tell that he was head over heels in love with her. As Lewis cuddled up to Martha, he said, "How about coming to my place for dinner tomorrow night, so I can show you around the place.

My mother and I just used the first floor and, after she died, I just continued that habit. There are several rooms on the second floor that you may want to use, but we'll have to make some changes. I know—you can do your vintage thing."

"My vintage thing?" Martha responded as she scowled at Lewis.

"Sorry, I don't know what to call it, but, you know, you love vintage and now you'll have an opportunity to do it on a large scale. I didn't mean to insult you, love, you know that—at least I hope you do."

"Lewis that's a great idea. So, I just may marry you after all," Martha said as she chuckled. "By the way, Lewis, I've been meaning to ask you—if Cora and your mother were sisters, how come you never refer to the Worthingtons as aunt and uncle."

"There's a long story about that, and I think it's time that I explain how and why I wound up living at the Worthington compound. When WWII exploded, my dad was drafted into the army. I have no memories of him. He died on Omaha Beach. Unfortunately, my mom was never able to function when she lost him. Cora managed to talk her into moving to one of the houses on the Worthington compound, where she could keep a close eye on her. It didn't take long for Matthew and me to become buddies, even though he was almost four years younger than I. When the two of us ran around together, I wanted to be one of the ordinary guys, so I never told anyone that Matthew and I were related. Then, later on, I didn't want our clients to know either, so I talked to Ronald about that and he said it was fine with him; in fact, he praised me for my business sense. So, I always tried to keep separate my public life from my private life."

"Did you two attend the same schools?"

"Just about. I got an MBA from Stanford. I went on to earn my PhD. I owe all of that to Ronald and Cora. I must add, however, that Matthew was a much more devoted student than I was. But, I really believe that I'm much more dogmatic when it comes to reeling in clients. I've put all my energy into my job. I wanted Cora and Ronald to be proud of me. They have also provided me with *the* model of what a healthy, happy marriage is, my darling, and that's why I chose you."

"It's obvious that they adore you. You know, you and I have been completely devoted to our jobs. And whether we realized it not, we were also searching for our soul mates."

Their conversation turned to various aspects of Lewis's life. Martha realized that her knowledge of Lewis' interests had many blank spaces. "I would like to know little things about you. For instance, I don't know your favorite color, or what kind of music you like."

"Of course, my favorite color is green," he said as he put his finger under her chin and lifted her face up to look into her eyes. "What other color is there? And, as for music, you'll never guess—its big band music from the forties. My grandmother used to play her records for me when I was a kid. Now, however, my favorite music is anything that's being played while I'm dancing with you."

'What about hobbies?"

"When I was about fifteen, Ronald took me with him one day when visiting an important business friend. When we got to his office, we were ushered into another room where his friend was playing on a billiards table. I watched in amazement as the man was able to hit one ball, while knocking three others into different pockets on the table. Later, when I found a bar with a pool table and I was allowed to use a cue stick, I knew that I had found a genuine interest. When my mom found out, she told me that only riff-raff played pool. Matthew never told anyone that I would often sneak away and play pool. I have a billiards table in my house where Matthew and I play whenever he's in the States. Would you like to learn how to shoot pool?"

"Lewis, you never cease to amaze me. It seems as if I'm learning something new about you every day."

"Martha, now about the wedding. Or, are you deliberately avoiding the topic?"

"I'm not sure I'm ready to talk about that. I think I need to speak with Cora first."

"Okay, but let me give you some ideas. First, we could elope. Or, we could jump on a plane, fly to Vegas, and get married at a little chapel. Or, we could have a big wedding and let Reggie be the ring bearer. He would look great in a little velvet suit, carrying a pillow with our wedding rings on," Lewis said as he laughed.

Elaine appeared and said, "Prepare for landing," as she made certain that they had fastened their seat belts.

"After all the excitement we have had, it may be nice to settle down to an everyday life," Martha said.

As they went through immigration, they could see Rocco walking back and forth in the screened-off area.

"Rocco, you look perturbed. Is something wrong?"

"Folks, let's go over there. We need to talk," Rocco said solemnly.

As he relayed what had happened in Martha's home, Martha grabbed Lewis' arm. "My God! Why? What did I do?"

"Martha, a restoration company is working on your home as we speak. It will take some time, but the damage will be repaired. We're not sure whether the target is really you—it could be Lewis," Rocco explained.

Lewis put his arm around Martha. "Sweetheart, you'll stay with me. Rocco, can Martha get in her house now to get clothing and other essentials?"

"Sure, we can do that."

"Martha, from now on, you will have two assigned drivers. Unless Rocco or I are at the wheel, you will not get in any car, no matter what the driver may tell you. This is vital—as soon as we catch this bastard, we can make other arrangements," Lewis said firmly.

⋙ CHAPTER 25 ⋘

April 18, 1972

"DID EVERYTHING GO alright when Rocco drove you around to your four libraries today?" Lewis asked as he took off his suit coat.

"Fine. He's such a patient person. Stanley would have kept him all day at his library. When he discovered that Rocco was a Phillies fan, Stanley was in seventh heaven. He finally had someone to talk with about baseball. They all liked the little china bells I bought in Haworth for them—even Stanley," Martha said. "By the way, we're due at Winnie's place by six. I really appreciate your being willing to go along. I know that she can be a bit chatty, but she's such a dear friend."

"No problem," Lewis said as he put on a cardigan sweater. "Will this be okay?"

"Sure. Winnie said that it will be just the three of us. I know that she's going to have lots of questions—you know, the trip, the engagement, and the destruction done at my place."

As they drove to Winnie's, Lewis said, "I'm glad you like Rocco because I really don't know how long we're going to have to do this, but it's vital that we keep you protected."

"I'm really disturbed that someone could call me such a

vile name. I don't think I'll ever forget what was written on my living room wall."

"They did that to hurt you—don't let them succeed. I'm more certain each day that I'm the target and not you."

"You think it could be someone you did business with? But, if they were unhappy, wouldn't they try a business tactic, instead?"

"Well, it could be. But, let's not mention our fears to Winnie. We don't want her to worry about being collateral damage," Lewis said as he entered Winnie's driveway.

Winnie was standing in the doorway. "Let me see—let me see," she said as she tried to get a look at Martha's ring. "Oh, my God, Lewis, that's a beautiful ring. You have great taste," she said as she kissed Martha's cheek, and then grabbed Lewis and planted a kiss on his cheek, too.

As they sat around the dinner table, Winnie continued her questioning. After they covered the how, when, and where of the proposal, the topic immediately went to the damage done to Martha's home.

"Do the police have any suspects?"

"I'm sure they do, but they play their cards close to their chests. They are, however, eager to get their hands on a photograph album that Martha had purchased at Nickles some time ago. But, it disappeared," Lewis explained. "The album is supposed to contain photos of some of the actors that appeared in summer stock shows. In my young and dumb days, I used to hang around those people, so I know a few of them."

"Can't they just get pictures from the theater where they performed?" Winnie asked.

"It could be that there's something else in the album. That

may be why they broke into Martha's home. They could have been hunting for the album."

Winnie dropped her fork. "The album will help Martha?"

"We think so …"

Winnie jumped up and left the room. When she returned, she was carrying the album in her hands. "Here," she said as she laid it in front of Lewis.

Martha and Lewis were astounded. But, when Winnie began to cry, Martha went to her side. "Winnie, it will be alright. Don't cry," she said as she wrapped her arms around her friend. "You've done us a large favor. We thought that it was gone for good—you did the right thing."

Lewis opened the album. "Here's McKnight." Slipping the photo out of the gold corners, he turned it over.

Martha was holding her breath. "Do you see any writing?"

"Definitely. It's faded, but I think with the right equipment, we'll be able to see what someone wrote."

CHAPTER 26

April 19, 1972

CHIEF WEAVER LEANED back in his chair, put his glasses on, and said, "Okay, Holmes, let's go over this again. Miss Harrison purchased a photograph album at Nickles some time ago. She was intrigued by it since the album had belonged to Dorothy Evans. Then it disappeared, but no one bothered to tell the police. The photo album—which you couldn't find before—suddenly appeared at your doorstep. Who put it there? Perhaps it was the Tooth Fairy, or maybe the Easter Bunny," Weaver said sarcastically.

"I haven't the foggiest idea who put it there, but when I came out of my house last night, there it was. Just like that," Lewis said, knowing full well that the Chief was not buying his story.

"I wonder why the album wasn't placed at Miss Harrison's doorstep, rather than yours," Weaver said as he peered over the top of his glasses at Lewis. Interviewing the nephew of one of the richest men in the state was a challenge that he would have preferred to avoid. "You know that we have reopened the Dorothy Evans' murder case, and that we're looking for an album that she supposedly kept on the actors who, at one time or another, appeared in summer stock shows. Magically, it falls from the damned sky and lands on your property. Okay, let's say I believe your story. Now, tell me—which of these people did you know?" he asked as he began to tap his foot on the floor, while tossing photos across the table to Lewis.

"Well, this is Howard McKnight. We used to be friends until he caught Rosa Gonzales and me making out at a party. He got pissed off because, at the time, Rosa and he were supposedly a couple. Howard was a good-looking guy— definitely had movie star looks, except that he had huge teeth. From the stage, his smile looked good. But close up, his teeth were oversized and made him look like a beaver. From then on, I guess I became a bully. He irritated me so much that I used to walk around with my upper lip pulled back and my teeth showing, trying hard to imitate a beaver. He would get livid. One day, he jumped over the table and tried to stab me with a pocket knife. I was a nineteen-year-old brat until Ronald straightened me out. When I stopped running around with the summer stock crowd, I lost touch with him. And, this is Rosa," Lewis explained, as he tapped a photo. "Oh, Howard taught me how to shoot pool, so I guess I should be grateful for that. He was just not a good actor...or a nice person."

"Back then, McKnight was the prime suspect, but he had a solid alibi. It seems that he was somewhere in Africa shooting scenes for a movie," Weaver explained. "The case then went cold. Tell me about Gonzales."

"She was a dark-haired beauty and she bounced from one guy to another. Howard may have believed he and Rosa were a couple, but she had different ideas. She got around quite a bit. Her parents supposedly owned a thriving restaurant in LA and eventually she went back. I think she left sometime before Dorothy was murdered. She couldn't have participated in the crime. That's all I know."

"Okay, Holmes, you may go now. I might be calling you back, so don't plan any overseas trips for a while," the Chief ordered. "I understand that you and Miss Harrison are engaged. When you see her, tell her I'll be interviewing her before too long."

"Oh, come on now, Weaver. Martha didn't know any of these people."

"Maybe so, but she had the album at one time. Now, get out of here and thanks for bringing the album in," Weaver said as politely as he was able.

Later that afternoon, one of the department's detectives made a few calls and, in almost no time at all, had located Rosa Gonzales. "You won't believe this, Chief, but she's right in the next county, teaching an ESL course in a private school. And, she's willing to come in Monday for an interview."

"Great. Contact Miss Harrison and schedule her, too, for Monday. We'll see how that goes and then we'll probably go after McKnight. I'm going to get to the bottom of this case before I retire. If Holmes thinks I believed that cockamamie story he gave me, he ought to have his damned head examined."

"Are you looking at Holmes as a possible suspect?"

"Right now, they're all suspects. Now, get the hell out of here and check on whether anyone can read the writing on the back of the photo of McKnight. Africa, or no Africa, I still like him as a prime suspect."

While all of this was happening, Martha had gone up to the second floor of Lewis' home to look around. When she opened the first door, she was dumbfounded. Before her eyes were shelves and shelves of books. Much to her delight, the furniture was vintage. By a row of windows, two wingback chairs complemented a lower credenza filled with still more books. She stood for several minutes just letting her eyes take in the names on the spines of the books. Someone, at some time, had taken loving care of these treasures. Daphne du Maurer, Charles Dickens, Virginia Woolf, George Orwell, Oscar Wilde, and Shakespeare were just a few of the names she saw on the spines.

As she pulled the door shut, she took her time in surveying the room. In the one corner was a marble-topped table, holding a classic stained-glass lamp she thought might be Tiffany. Two eye-catching landscape oil paintings were hanging on either side of a cherry library table. In the far corner was a marble bust of Mark Twain. On one hand, she wanted to shout out with joy, but, on the other, she didn't want to break the emotional roller-coaster that she was on just looking around the fabulous room.

She moved closer to the books. Running her hands over them, she recalled the little library she had had in her bedroom before she had to live with Aunt Ivy. The only word that she could think of at the moment to describe her findings was *bonanza.* She could bring this room back to life,

As she was surveying the sight, she noticed that on the right-hand side of the book shelves, several books seemed to be jutting out just a bit too far. Spying a small stepstool, she used it to reach them. She smiled when she saw that the books were collections of short stories by Edgar Allan Poe, one of her favorite authors. She immediately thought about some of the gruesome topics Poe explored—a beating heart buried beneath the floor board, a black cat that exposes a murder, and a barrel of wine that causes a man to be buried alive— ugh. Pulling a few of them sown, she was surprised to see a lever. When she instinctively pulled on it she was knocked off the stool onto the floor as the wall opened up to reveal a hidden room. She pulled herself up again and took a closer look at the lever.

Rocco called to her when he heard a thump. Quickly, she pushed the lever to close the opening. She wanted to surprise Lewis. He had to be the first one that she wanted to share this unbelievable experience with.

Rocco came rushing in the library. "Martha, did you fall? I thought I heard a noise."

"I slipped off the stool. I think I twisted my foot a bit."

Rocco examined her foot and said, "I don't think anything's broken, but just to be safe, I'm going to take you to the doctor."

"I have to say *no* to that. I'm okay. I want to keep working on these books, Rocco," Martha said, hardly able to contain her excitement. She would tell Lewis first and then she'd tell Cora. What a day, she thought—vintage furniture, a classic library, and a secret room. What could top this?

⋙ CHAPTER 27 ⋘

April 20, 1972

A S LEWIS HURRIED up the stairway and into the second floor library, he said, "Hello, Green Eyes. How's the foot coming along?"

"Lewis, I'm fine. Rocco brought me a wheelchair that I hought I didn't need, but it has come in handy and allows me to keep off my foot. I simply wheel myself back and forth with the books in my lap."

"According to the piles of books I see on that table, you have been a busy librarian. Find anything interesting?" he asked as he wrapped his arms around her.

"Lewis, stay right there," she said as she walked over to the bookshelves. "Now, watch this." She pulled the lever to open the door to the secret room.

Lewis' eyes opened wide. "How did you find that?"

"When I noticed some books jutting out further than the others, I pulled them out and there was the lever—so I pulled it."

"I can't imagine that I lived in this house for years and never knew about that. Did you go inside the room?"

"No. I wasn't brave enough to do that," Martha said as she laughed.

Lewis walked over to the opening. "I'll have to duck a bit, but I've got to see where this goes. Those skylights should provide enough light," he said as he stepped over the sill.

In less than a minute, he was back. "It's like a wide hallway that curves to the right, but I don't see an exit of any kind, unless that's hidden, too. You know, this area is famous for being part of the Underground Railroad. Several homes were used as *safe houses.* Do you think our house could have been part of the network established by the abolitionists?"

"We need to get Ronald and Cora over here. They might know," Martha suggested.

Lewis went to the stairway and called to Rocco. "Hey, Rocco, call Ronald. Tell him that we would like to see Cora and him as soon as possible. If they're available, please drive them over here. Thanks."

"Okay, Boss."

"If I would have known about that room when I was a kid growing up here, I would have played in there all the time," Lewis said. "Martha, you are amazing. Did you learn about secret rooms when you were in your library classes?" Lewis joked.

"Of course not, silly. I'm naturally curious. But, let me tell you something else. This is a great collection of books. We have excellent resources to help our children learn about good literature."

"Young lady," he said, "are you trying to seduce me. I hope."

They were interrupted by Ronald's voice, who good-naturally was chiding Lewis. "This better be good, Lewis, I was watching a game," Ronald said as he climbed the stairs.

"Ronnie, you were taking a nap. Now, hush, Lewis needs to see us," Cora said gently.

As the two of them spied the opening to the secret room, they were stunned.

"Come," Lewis said as he took Ronald's arm and led him to the entrance.

When they came out, Ronald said, "I'll be damned. I used to hear stories about the Underground Railroad, but I thought they were just that—stories. But you may be right, Lewis. I think I'll contact Jim Luckenbill, over at the college, and ask him to do some research on this place. I'd like to believe that my ancestors were abolitionists."

⤳ CHAPTER 28 ⤤

April 24, 1972

CHIEF WEAVER HURRIED into his office and looked for a brown manila envelope that would hold the lab results on enhancing the writing on McKnight's photograph. Eureka! It was there. He held his breath as he slid the report out of the envelope and read it quickly. It was all he needed to bring McKnight to Logan County and, hopefully, to lock him up for good. Apparently, young Dorothy Evans had been pregnant and had expected the father of the child to marry her. In Dorothy's own handwriting, she claimed that McKnight refused to walk down the aisle unless she had an abortion. Wow!

Weaver picked up his phone. "Kenneth, call our contact at the LAPD and ask them to pick up McKnight. When we know for sure that they have him in custody, you and Bert fly out there and bring that bastard in." He hadn't liked McKnight when he met him years ago. His instincts had been right. "Meanwhile, Kenneth, as soon as Miss Gonzales arrives, bring her to my office."

When his office door opened, and Rosa Gonzales stepped in, he was pleasantly surprised—she was indeed a beauty. He hurriedly stood up, shook her hand, and said, "Thank you so much for coming in, Miss Gonzales."

"I'm not certain that I'll be able to help you. While I knew Dorothy, we were not buddies. But, from time to time, she would share her love life problems with me—you know—it was usually just girl talk."

"Did she have, let's say, a steady boyfriend?"

"She had an eye for Lewis Holmes, but I don't think that went anywhere. Right before I decided to go back to LA, she was dating Howard McKnight. But, they were on again, off again, if you know what I mean. I dated McKnight one time. That was enough. He was such an egotist that I couldn't stand him. Sometimes, I saw a look in his eyes that made me think that ice water ran through his veins. I remember that it made me shudder."

Weaver then pulled out several photographs from his desk drawer and handed them to Rosa. "Do you know any of these people?"

After looking the photos over, Rosa replied, "I'm sorry, Chief Weaver, I don't. I was only in this part of the country for several weeks."

"Thank you, Miss Gonzales," Weaver said as he stood up.

"I guess I shouldn't say this, but—I do believe that McKnight was twisted enough to kill Dorothy, cut her up in pieces, and stuff her in a suitcase. He always seemed to love the macabre—the more gruesome a scene was, the more he enjoyed it. He frequently put on presentations designed to shock the general public."

As Rosa headed for the front door, she screamed when he spied Lewis sitting on a bench. Paying no attention to the woman who was sitting with him, Rosa threw her arms around Lewis and yelled excitedly, "Mopsy! My God, Lewis, I haven't seen you in years," she said as she kissed him on his lips.

"Rosa," a flustered Lewis said as he leaned down to take Martha's hand. "This is my gorgeous fiancée, Martha Harrison."

Turning to Martha, she said, "Congratulations. He was a bit young for us. He would lollygag behind us, along with his cousin, whom we called Flopsy. You know—Flopsy, Mopsy, and Cotton Tail from Beatrix Potter," Rosa said as she laughed.

"Miss Harrison, the Chief will see you now," a detective interrupted as he pointed to the correct office.

As Martha sat down across from Weaver, she said, "I really don't know if I can help you at all with this murder case." Still reeling from seeing Rosa kiss Lewis, Martha could only think of one thing and that was to get out of the Chief's office as quickly as she could.

Chief Weaver was beginning to believe that he had struck gold today. First, his lab was able to read what was on the back of McKnight's photo, then he interviewed the beautiful Rosa Gonzales, and now another charmer—this one with green eyes—was waiting to be interviewed. This job keeps getting better and better—maybe he might not retire at all.

"I understand that you had the Evans' album in your possession at one time," Weaver said. "How did that happen?"

"I love to shop at Nickles Vintage Treasures. One day, when I had noticed the album, and Mr. Nickles had told me that it had belonged to Dorothy Evans, I had been intrigued. I had felt sorry for her and had thought that I could take care of it for her even though I had never met the woman. You know, I just wanted to be nice," Martha explained. "I was heartbroken when it disappeared."

"Why didn't you report the theft to the police?"

"Lewis and I thought it would be better if whoever was

interested in the album would believe that we just didn't know that it was gone."

"How did McKnight's photo play a role in this mess?"

"On the day that I had bought the album, I also had purchased an antique picture frame that I had thought would look great on an end table in my living room. But I didn't have a photo to put in it. Then, I had remembered that one photo in the album appeared to be the exact size I needed, so I removed it and placed it in the frame as a temporary way to use the frame."

"Even though you didn't know the man?"

"I know it sounds silly, Chief, but I was after a vintage look. It wasn't until much later that Lewis told me he knew McKnight. That's all I know," Martha said, getting more eager to check on Rosa and Lewis, who were in the waiting room. "Are we finished?"

"No. Are you telling me that you can't think of anyone who would have slashed your tires and vandalized your home? Someone is targeting you."

"I can't imagine who that person could possibly be," Martha said as she started to become visually shaken.

"And then, someone wrecked one of the libraries under your supervision. I know that that case is under the jurisdiction of the Sheriff's office, but it, too, is probably connected to the other cases," Weaver said sharply. "Your life might be hanging in the balance."

"Lewis is providing me with protection."

"Well, I'm glad to hear that, Miss Harrison. I don't mean to frighten you, but until we can put all the pieces of this puzzle together, you need to be alert. Okay, Miss Harrison. Thanks for coming in," Weaver said as Martha rushed out his office door.

Her heart fell when she realized that the waiting room was empty. She found Lewis and Rosa in a deep conversation on the front steps of the courthouse. As soon as Lewis spied her, he hurried to her side. "How did it go?"

"Fine... I see that you were well taken care of," Martha said, trying hard not to sound like a jealous shrew.

"Martha," Rosa said, "what a gorgeous bride you're going to be. Lewis, you're a lucky man. Now, I must run. I have a class to teach at two."

Martha finally smiled. Rosa was gone.

⇜ CHAPTER 29 ⇝

April 25, 1972

EARLY THE NEXT day, Chief Weaver was already planning on holding a press conference once he knew that McKnight was on his way back to Logan County. He wanted to solve this case so that he could leave the department while the praise would be rolling in. He had a pretty good idea who the mayor would appoint as the next chief and he really didn't like her at all. Besides, this was his baby and he hadn't submitted a formal resignation as yet.

As soon as Kenneth saw Weaver coming in the door, he rushed to his side. He whispered, "They can't find him."

"What the hell do you mean, *they can't find him*?" Weaver blustered.

"He had promised them that he would turn himself in as soon as he was finished shooting a scene and that they could expect him before eight last night. He never showed."

"What? Must I do everything myself? With this guy's reputation he could be anywhere in the world by now. So, here we are, ready to crack this case wide open and LA can't find him?" Weaver reached into his desk drawer and pulled out a bottle of aspirin and quickly tossed two of them down his throat. "We'll go the route of an APB. Print his picture and get it on WRCY immediately. My gut tells me that this guy's a son-of-a-bitch, so who knows where he'll surface."

Later that afternoon, Mookey was shaken when he saw McKnight's picture on the news. He had always suspected that his boss had killed that girl even though he had denied it time and time again. When Fat Tony came rushing in the front door shouting, "Mookey, Mookey, what the hell's going on?" Mookey's headache worsened. "I don't wanna to be drug into any murder. You promised we'd only be doin' crappy things, not murder."

"We didn't even know Mack when he killed that girl years ago. We both know that he wanted that librarian, Martha what's-her-name, to be afraid and on edge. The only one that I think he could be after is Lewis Holmes. I don't think Mack would be nuts enough to come here and try to get Holmes himself."

What are we gonna do?" Fat Tony said nervously.

"We're gonna stay put. If he don't show up, we'll be in the clear."

⪻ CHAPTER 30 ⪼

April 26, 1972

L EWIS PROPPED HIMSELF up in bed and watched Martha as she slept. He never got tired of doing this. As she stirred, he brushed the hair away from her face. She smiled. "My love," she whispered.

"There's a line from *War and Peace* that I'm sure you know—*we are asleep until we fall in love.* That fits me to a tee. Martha, I should write a thank-you letter to Leo Tolstoy for giving me such beautiful words to say to you."

"That's odd, I came across some words yesterday that reminded me of you when I was reading to the children in Gwen's library."

"Were you reading *Humpty Dumpty*?" Lewis kidded.

Martha sat up. "No, I was reading *Winnie the Pooh. As soon as I saw you, I knew an adventure was going to happen.* I only knew you for a few minutes when you tossed me to the floor. Lewis, you're the best thing that has ever happened to me. Even Winnie the Pooh knew that."

"I usually don't throw women onto the floor—just women with green eyes. I wanted to check them out to see if they were real," Lewis said as he laughed.

"You may have saved my life that night. You know what

else I think about that happened that night—our visit to the diner. Our little conversation was so precious—so inviting that I felt the doors to our very souls opened and we walked in. I love you, Lewis."

"I just might stay here all day if you promise to repeat those words."

"If my memory is right, you have a meeting scheduled in an hour with your staff about Matthew's Charity Day," she reminded him.

As Lewis got out of bed, he leaned down and kissed Martha. "You're right. He wants to have a party for his parents on Kentucky Derby Day that has a special meaning for them. Cora and Ronald met when Cora won a contest about the derby and was invited to a party held at Bella Luna. He looked at her, she looked at him, and the rest was history. And, the next year, on Derby Day, they were married. We were thinking about canceling the celebration when McKnight went missing, but since it's been three weeks and there haven't been any sightings of the bastard, we decided to go ahead with the party."

"I understand that there's going to be all kinds of games going on. What do you suggest for me?"

"There's a fun game using wooden horses you may like. Oh, and there's going to be a team trivia contest; you'll be dynamite at that. By the way, Rocco will take you to work today—just in case. Then, tomorrow, he'll drive you to Bella Luna around three when the festivities begin. There will be bar service in the ballroom. Food will be in the Rose Room and the dining room. But, please don't walk over to the mansion without Rocco."

"Lewis, when can we stop using Rocco as my protector? It makes me feel a little silly," Martha said.

"When it's safe and not before, Green Eyes."

"Tell me how Charity Day earns money."

"Well, when you decide on a game to play, you'll fill out a pledge form, stating how much you are donating to get in that game. Let's say you decide to get in the trivia contest. First, you fill out your pledge and give it to the Master of the Games, who will escort you to a seat. Oh, by the way, just pledge five thousand each time you play. If your team wins, each member of the team has the right to use the pledge of a losing team member for his or her favorite charity. Martha, don't be afraid to bet. We have the money to cover this. Remember, you'll be in the Worthington family, too, and it will be expected that you'll be generous at these events."

"What about the Kentucky Derby? Are we allowed to bet on that? I don't know anything about horses. But Winnie said she likes Riva Ridge."

"Since Reggie will be in charge of Derby bets, he'll be delighted to help you. I want you to have a good time. Look, I realize that Winnie can't afford this event, so how about that we give her several pledge forms that will be billed to me. That way, the two of you can have fun together. I'll be busy fighting off challengers at the billiards table."

"Lewis, Winnie the Pooh was right. You are an adventure every day," Martha said as she kissed him.

CHAPTER 31

May 6, 1972 7a.m.

H E SHUDDERED AS he stepped onto the linoleum-covered floor. He hated these damned seedy motels, but he had to watch his money carefully. He looked into the mirror and smiled. "What a handsome fellow you are, McKnight," Howard said to himself. He slipped on his tortoise-shell sunglasses and mangy pork pie hat. There was a completely new McKnight looking back at him.

When the LA Police Department called him to come in for an interview, a couple of weeks ago, he knew immediately that it was about that trollop, Dorothy Evans. There was no way in hell that he was going to prison for her death. The skinny, low-class broad had gotten pregnant, so that she could trap him. When he first had told her to get an abortion, she had refused. So, he promised that if she had an abortion, they would get married. He had told her that his father was against premarital sex, so, if there was no baby, the wedding could go on. She had readily agreed. He had taken her to a woman who lived in Raven Alley who specialized in getting rid of such problems. She was known as *Shady Lady*. Of course, later, when he let it slip to Dorothy that he was not going to marry her, she had threatened to tell his father. There had been a fight and he had strangled her.

He had dissected her and put her body parts into a suitcase. He then had visited *Shady Lady* once again who had readily agreed to dispose of the suitcase for a sum of money. He had felt free from the whole problem for a while. So, the cops can poke their noses around all they like, but there was no evidence against him. *Shady Lady* had died a few years ago. But, just in case they might have something against him, he was going to also get rid of Lewis Holmes—geez, he despised that guy. Besides, Dorothy used to run to Lewis Holmes with her personal problems and Howard couldn't be sure what that damned rich boy might know.

His hatred for Lewis had festered like a rotten, oozing wound. How dare that kid make fun of him and his looks? While Lewis might be the nephew of a rich man, he had no theatrical talent. Howard knew that he was a natural on the stage and his looks were part of his persona. Clark Gable, had a special look, too. Who could forget Gable watching Vivian Leigh climb that beautiful staircase in *Gone with the Wind?* He turned to look in the mirror. He still had that *it* factor, while Lewis had nothing. Lewis had turned Rosa against him—and, as a result, he had gotten involved with Dorothy. Things hadn't turned out the way he had planned and it was all Lewis' fault and HE WAS GOING TO PAY1.

He had been working on the script that he was going to use to get into Bella Luna without any problems. If he should lose the battle with Lewis Holmes, so be it. He would still go down in history as a man with a superior brain. Most people just assumed that they had to survive in whatever situation was handed to them—they were so wrong. What such morons didn't realize was that someone else might be inserting a new reality for them without their being aware that their real reality was no longer functioning. He smiled broadly when he thought about how clever he had been with tossing challenges at Lewis' lady love without either one of them realizing that someone, far smarter, was behind their every move.

This was the day—the day that he would achieve his highest goal—the day others would talk about in the years ahead. He had to time his arrival at the entrance gate after the local television station had been in place for at least a half hour. Not only was he a genius at film making, Howard knew that he was also a great actor. It would be like taking candy from a baby. Besides, today he had a much larger knife in his pocket.

He pulled directly up to the service gate at the rear of Bella Luna. He had his radio blasting away just to add to the casual look he was aiming for. The guard had a clipboard in his hand and was looking it over when Howard lowered the sound on his radio. "I was supposed to come in behind WRCV to do some filming for Charity Day, but I got caught in traffic down around where that new shopping mall is. Hey, those pictures you have on your counter, are they your kids?"

"Yeah, they are," the guard said proudly.

"Kids sure change your world, don't they? I can't let my boss know that I got lost getting here or I might lose my job," Howard said as he picked up his clip board. "I got a call from someone, let's see, oh yes, a Lewis Holmes, who wants me to do some filming. You know this guy?"

"Oh, I sure do. A hellava nice guy. Do you want me to call the station to let them know that you're running late?" the guard offered.

"I'd appreciate it very much if you didn't. If you can just guide me to where I can find Holmes, I can get in and have the filming done by noon and I'll earn brownie points from the boss. By the way, would you mind if I filmed you? I think it would be a nice opening for viewers to see such a handsome man. Like, you could pose alongside the photos of your kids. They would get a blast if they saw themselves on television," Howard said convincingly.

"That sounds great. You want to do that now?" the guard asked.

Howard jumped out of his truck, slung his camera on his shoulders, and in less than five minutes, the filming was completed.

"When you come to White Birch Lane, make a left and the first house you come to on the right is where Holmes lives," the guard said as he waved McKnight through the gate.

As he passed others, who were walking around, he waved to each one. Everyone appeared to be in a good mood. After all, it was Charity Day and that meant the food and drink would flow for hours. When he spotted Holmes' residence, he became concerned when he spotted some guy sitting on the porch steps. His first thought was to play it cool.

"Hi," McKnight said in a friendly manner, "I think I'm at the right place. I got orders from Mr. Lewis Holmes to do some pre-party filming at his home."

"You're at the right place, buddy. I'm not sure he's home, but I know that Martha's in the library on the second floor," Rocco said.

McKnight hurried up the porch steps and into the house. He moved to the stairway and climbed them as quietly as he could. All the doors were closed. Then he heard some music. He followed the sound and opened the door. He saw her in person for the first time. Good looking woman. Now, she was seated in a wheelchair with lots of books piled on her lap. He cleared his throat, so she would know that he had entered the room.

Martha looked up from the wheelchair that she was using to move books from one shelf to another. She saw the smile—that mile with perfect teeth that she had looked at so many times—it was McKnight, with cameras slung over his shoulders. She knew that his photo had been on television and that the police were looking for him. Her thoughts raced from wondering why he was at their house to why Rocco had not stopped him from coming up the stairway. But her gut told her that he wanted Lewis—she had to be smart enough—clever enough—not to let that happen. Don't panic. Play your best role—the accommodating Book Lady. She realized that her button to sound the alarm was on the other side of the room. She knew instinctively that she could not let him know that she knew who he was. Lewis—I must protect Lewis, who was downstairs meeting with his staff.

"Hello," Martha said as she continued to flip through the books. "I didn't know about any filming taking place here for Charity Day. I'm a mess right now. I apologize for that."

As McKnight smiled, Martha held her breath.

"Is Lewis Holmes here?" McKnight asked.

"He's in the billiards room. He's practicing his shots since he's going to be challenged by lots of others to raise money for charity today."

"If you direct me, I'll film him first," McKnight said a bit too eagerly.

"Well, I can show you a short cut to the billiards room. Now, keep your eyes on the wall," she said as she pulled the lever to reveal the secret room.

"I'll be damned," McKnight said.

"You can just cut through here and when you get to the end

of the hallway, you'll find a pedal on the floor to open the door to the billiards room. Lewis will be totally surprised when you show up," Martha said sweetly. "Lewis loves surprises."

"Thanks, ma'am," McKnight said as he stepped into the room. "Perhaps you should go with me," he said cautiously.

"I'd love to, but I can't get out of this chair. I sprained my foot the other day and the chair's too wide to get in there. Have fun," she said, delighted at her performance. She counted to five and then pulled the lever to close the wall. In no time at all, McKnight was stomping around like a maniac, screaming and yelling obscenities.

She hurriedly pressed the alarm button. Rocco came bounding up the stairs. Lewis was a few steps behind.

"What is it, Martha, what's wrong?" Lewis said loudly.

"McKnight," she said breathlessly. "He's in the secret room."

"My God, Martha. How in the hell did you do that?" Lewis asked as he put his arms around her.

All the while, McKnight had apparently lost all control and his fear of closed spaces took over. He screamed, "Get me out—get me out!"

When Lewis' staff realized what had happened, they were surprisingly quiet. "Hey, guys, don't feel bad, as long as we have Martha on our side, we're okay."

"Martha, does he have a gun?" Rocco asked.

"I'm not sure."

"How did you recognize him?" Lewis asked.

"That perfect smile with perfect teeth," she said as she laughed.

"Martha, get out of here. We're going in there to drag him out. Stay out until we have him cuffed," Lewis ordered.

"Rocco, I think he's claustrophobic. So, we'll open the

door, but he won't see any of us. His fear will bring him out. Everyone but Rocco and Lewis left the room. As soon a Lewis pulled the lever to open the door, he slid under the desk. In a few minutes McKnight staggered out of the secret room. He was sobbing and clutching at his clothing. Lewis and Rocco tackled him easily and put him in handcuffs.

Just then, Chief Weaver walked into the room. McKnight was on the floor, sobbing like a child, while Rocco and Lewis stood there smiling. Weaver spotted the secret room and began to put the pieces together. "Who the hell got him to go in there?"

"The Book Lady," they all shouted.

"Holy hell, he must have owed a lot of overdue book fines," Weaver said as he laughed at his own joke.

No one took notice of the beat-up station wagon that drove past the police cars. Fat Tony slouched down in his seat and pulled a knit cap over his face.

"Hey, they ain't looking for you, so why are you hiding? Just act natural and we'll be in Canada before you know it," Mookey said sharply. "My cousin will take us in and we'll stay there until Mack goes to prison. Meanwhile, stop acting so dumb, or I'll toss you out at the first rest stop we come to."

⇜ CHAPTER 32 ⇝

May 6, 1972 3 p.m.

As the guests were arriving to celebrate Charity Day at Bella Luna, they were surprised to see so many cars driving away. Winnie was sitting in her car waiting to get in, all the while clutching her gold embossed invitation. Her heart was in her throat. It was the first time that she was visiting the mansion. However, what excited her the most was that she would be mingling with rich and famous people. Nervously, she pulled up to the guard who had a clipboard in his hand.

"Hello, Miss, name please," said the guar, as he smiled at Winnie.

"Winnie Carson."

The guard looked over the list and then said, "Drive right in Miss Carson. May I ask: Who do you like in the Derby?"

"I think I'll bet on RIVA RIDGE."

"Good choice, Miss. Have a great day."

There were more attendants lined up along the driveway, directing drivers to various parking lots. She was amazed at the size of everything—big and expensive, she thought. As she opened her car door, a gentleman came over and offered his hand. She found herself looking into the deepest brown eyes she had ever seen. "Thank you," Winnie managed to say.

It was just a little after three, so she hoped that Martha was waiting for her since she didn't know what to do next. "Miss, just follow those people going in that door and that will take you directly to the ballroom." This Prince Charming had a voice that sent shivers up her spine.

Much to her relief, Martha was waiting for Winnie and showed her where all the games were taking place. "Winnie, these are pledge sheets that you use when you get in a game. Each one is worth five thousand. When you win a game, then you get to pull out a pledge sheet from the barrel and pick the charity that will get the money."

"My God, Martha, I can't afford that," Winnie said as she swallowed hard.

"Not to worry. Lewis paid for them. He wants you to have a good time. Besides, he wants to donate the money to charity. Just have fun."

Winnie's response was silenced as Ronald walked across the stage and approached the microphone. "Before we begin our Charity Day party, I have something to share with you. As you know from the news, the police have been looking for a suspect in the Dorothy Evans' murder case. His name is Howard McKnight. McKnight used his skills as an actor to get into Bella Luna today."

The guests all looked at one another and began whispering.

"However, you need not worry. Thanks to the skills and courage of someone in this room, McKnight is currently behind bars in our local jail."

The crowd began clapping. Then, they started asking, "Who?"

"Was it Lewis?" someone shouted.

Ronald smiled. "No, not Lewis. But you're getting closer. It was the Book Lady of Bella Luna, Lewis' intended, Martha

Harrison." The crowd cheered. "When I told her that I was going to let you know what happened, she asked me not to. But, Martha, this world needs more heroines like you. Thank you. Oh, Chief Weaver also asked me to thank you once again. Now, I'll turn this over to our son Matthew."

"Thank you for coming to Charity Day, which is always held on the day that the Kentucky Derby runs at Churchill Downs. This is also the day that I want to honor my parents. Back in 1931, my mom entered a radio contest and the prize was an invitation to Bella Luna for a Derby Day party. Well, she won the prize. When she arrived, she was greeted by three handsome men: my Uncle Reggie; Gregory, their cousin; and of course my dad, Ronald. He looked at my mom, she looked at him, and the rest was history.

"My parents and I want to announce that very shortly there will be the sound of little feet at Bella Luna—my family and I will be coming back here to live at the end of May. My wife, Patricia, our sons, Matthew, Jr., Mark, and Michael, and our daughter Miranda will finally be home—hopefully for good."

Cora jumped to her feet and applauded.

'Mom, remember, don't spoil them too much," Matthew cautioned. "Now, on to the party. Mom, I have some questions for you. Who won the Derby the day you stepped in Bella Luna and met dad?"

Cora called out, "Twenty Grand."

"Mom, you and dad were married on Derby Day in 1932. Who won the Derby on that day?"

"That was BURGOO KING," she replied.

"Now, be careful with this one, mom. Who will win the Derby today?"

"RIVA RIDGE," she responded.

"You heard it from an expert. Uncle Reggie is taking the Derby bets. Folks, we encourage you to be generous with your pledges. We are welcoming several new charities this year. Open your hearts, open your pocketbooks, and get your pledges in. Thank you!"

Martha and Winnie began their adventure by entering a trivia contest. Then they played a variety of other games, winning two of them. Winnie was so excited when she pulled out a Pledge Sheet for ten thousand dollars. When the Master of the Games asked her where the money should go, she quickly picked the Children's Hospital."

When Martha decided to get in a poker game, Winnie said, "I think I'll just watch for a while. Go ahead, Martha. I want to look around."

Winnie began to circulate, trying to decide what she should play. Suddenly, there he was—Prince Charming. "By the way, my name is Anthony Caraballo." For the next several hours, Winnie was on cloud nine, laughing and talking and playing games with Anthony. Later, when the big screen was rolled out so that guests could watch the Kentucky Derby, they stood side by side, enjoying every moment.

"Winnie, are you going to bet on the Derby?" As she shook her head, Anthony waved at Reggie, who was taking Derby bets. "Reggie, this young lady and I wish to pledge five thousand on RIVA RIDGE. Winnie, when the Derby is over, dancing will begin. If RIVA RIDGE wins, you must have the first dance with me," Anthony said.

"And, if he loses, then what? Winnie asked.

"Oh, then you must also have the first dance with me. You see, I really don't care who wins the Derby, I just want the first dance with you."

When RIVA RIDGE entered the Winners' Circle at the

Derby, Anthony said, "Oh, I forgot, Winnie that means you must dance with me all night."

The night flew away. When Winnie finally spotted Martha, she pulled her aside. "Martha, that's Anthony Caraballo. Isn't he divine? I think I might have found the one."

Martha beamed, looked at Anthony, and said, "You have good taste, Rocco."

Rocco's smile said it all. He was enthralled with Winnie. Just then, Ronald walked over to Cora and extended his hand. "Cora, this old fool would love to dance with you."

"Well, this old fool says: What took you so long?" As the two of them collapsed in laughter, they put their arms around each other and lost themselves in the divine music.

Martha felt Lewis' arms go around her waist. "Lewis, look at them. Isn't true love wonderful?"

"Tell me all about it, Green Eyes."

Meanwhile, in Toronto, Mookey and Fat Tony were looking for a place to eat. "We gotta be careful with our dough. We gotta come up with an idea to make money."

They sat down on a bench along the sidewalk and Mookey counted their money. They both jumped when an alarm sounded. Mookey turned around.

"Holy hell, look out here comes a car like a bat out of hell."

The men who ran out of the store were anxious to get into the car. One was carrying a large bag while the other one had two smaller bags that he was trying to sling into the car when one dropped into the gutter right near Fat Tony's feet. Fat Tony reached down and scooped up the bag as he and Mookey ran down an alleyway. The car with the robbers sped away while the one in the back seat was pointing a gun at Fat Tony.

They took refuge in a dimly-lit parking garage and waited for silence from the streets. As Mookey looked into the bag, he said, "Jesus, look at this. We hit the jackpot. Gold and diamonds. These will get us far away from here."

When traffic came to a halt, they cautiously left the garage. "Mookey, my cousin can get us passports. How about going to Maui? I'm the one who picked up the bag, so it's my decision."

⫷ CHAPTER 33 ⫸

After the party 1 a.m.

Lewis and Martha were walking hand-in-hand by the lake. The moon was casting unique shadows across the water. Every once in a while, they would stop, embrace, and then kiss. When they came to their favorite bench, they sat down and cuddled even closer.

"You know, I can't remember much before I met you. I know that I worked and that I made a lot of money for Ronald. I think I enjoyed that, but I can't be sure. Now, every minute of the day, when I'm not with you, seems like an eternity until I have you back in my sight," Lewis said softly as he played with Martha's hair. "I guess I owe this to that guy who shot at us at the Holiday Hop. When you didn't dump me, when I threw you to the floor, I just knew that out of all the women in the world—and there are a lot of them—you were the one for me."

"Did they ever catch the man who shot at you that night?"

"Nope. But if we ever do, I'm going to shake his hand," Lewis said lightheartedly.

The Spring Peepers let everyone know that they were all around the lake with their high-pitched chirps. A slight breeze began to blow and Martha snuggled against Lewis as tightly as she could. "I never thought that I would be living in Bella Luna. It's changing—are you ready for that?"

"How do you see it changing?"

"For instance, in a few months, Matthew will be in charge. And there will be lots of children. Matthew's three sons and his daughter. Rocco will be in charge of Bella Luna security and, if Winnie and he became a couple, they will probably have children. Then, there will be our children."

"Oh yes, all twelve of them," Lewis added.

"Bella Luna will need a school bus," Martha laughed.

"Martha, how about Christmas Eve?"

"What about Christmas Eve?"

"Let's get married."

EPILOGUE

Ten years later.....

- Martha and Lewis have twin boys, who are 8 and a daughter who is 6.

- Winnie and Rocco have three daughters, who are 8, 6, and 5.

- Matthew's sons, ages 15, 11, and 10 and daughter, age 13, have assumed the roles as protectors of all the other children.

- Lewis, as CEO of the Ronald and Cora Worthington Foundation, has doubled its assets.

- Matthew has proven himself as an astute venture capitalist.

- Ronald Worthington purchased a mini-van for the children of Bella Luna to get to the elementary school and the academy.

- Howard McKnight is serving a life sentence for the murder of Dorothy Evans.

- Martha runs an after-school homework program in her little library.

- Martha and Mr. Nickles are partners in an online vintage Shop.

- Reggie Worthington married his fourth wife, who had been a Vegas showgirl.

- Stanley Barber won an award from the American Library Association as an outstanding Library Director.

- Mookey and Fat Tony are still being hunted by the Royal Canadian Mounted Police as well as the gang of thieves who want their bag of jewels back.

- Researchers have traced the creation of the secret room to the Underground Railroad.

Printed in the United States
By Bookmasters